JANA M. FLOYD

Paradise Valley

First edition

Editing by David G. Brown with Invisible Ink Editing
Cover art by Cover Art by Kellie Dennis at Book Cover by Design www.bookcoverbydesign.co.uk

This book was professionally typeset on Reedsy.
Find out more at reedsy.com

To Kaitlin and Jimmy -
You Know Why.

Contents

1. The Mud Puddle

Her hand slammed against the steering wheel, announcing her frustration not only to herself but also to the small rental car. Claire immediately stroked the car's dashboard in a soothing, loving apology. She didn't want to jinx anything; she was having bad enough luck as it was.

"I'm sorry, baby," she cooed. "It would just be nice if I knew where the hell I was."

She had been driving for two hours, but she had been covering the same stretch of road for the last thirty or forty minutes. Back and forth, back and forth over the packed dirt—Claire hardly considered it an actual road. The spiffy Smart-car was covered in a thick layer of fine Montana dust, and more than a few dead bugs decorated the windshield.

"Drive out to the ranch, they said," Claire muttered in a disgruntled voice. "It will be fun, they said. You'll get lots of work done, they said."

The directions to the "paradise" she booked for her "writing holiday" were balled up on the passenger floorboard of the car.

They had been smoothed and re-crumpled more than once since she had set out driving in this godforsaken place. The man had said they were precise instructions. Precise her ass. She had read them over dozens of times now, and she was no closer to the ranch than when she had left the Missoula Airport.

Claire reached down and tried to grab at the instructions. They were just out of her reach. She took her eyes off the road, only for a second, stretching her arm out like Gumby. Her fingertips brushed paper and she gripped it tightly.

"Ha!" Her triumphant hoot filled the tiny car. The small success filled her with adrenaline and confidence. She could take on the wilderness of Montana. That is, just as soon as she found the blasted ranch.

Claire looked back up to the road and caught a flash of fur skittering across the road. Her foot slammed on the brake automatically, and her scream echoed in the car as she came to a screeching halt, seatbelt locking to hold her in place.

Claire sat for a moment, dragging in deep breaths, trying to recover. There was no sign of whatever-animal the fur had belonged to.

"Go into the wilderness, they said…"

She hadn't even seen what kind of animal it was, not that she was likely to recognize it if she had. Unless it was a rat. Cities had rats. She definitely knew what rats looked like. But for all she knew, she could have just seen an evil buffalo or a moose that had apparently been trying to murder her. Which did seem a little rude, since it was her first visit to the Treasure State.

Her hands were only shaking a little as they smoothed out the hopelessly crinkled paper that contained the useless directions. Claire read the instructions over again, twice, out loud.

"Do they make sense to you?" she asked the car, only half

joking. Of course, it didn't answer. She sighed, resigned to her sad fate and said, "I guess we will just go back to the main highway and start over. Again."

Claire turned the car around and then laid her foot down on the gas pedal. The little car flew down the road, kicking up dust that seemed to have settled on the road from decades of neglect.

"It's probably not even a real place," Claire continued. "They took my deposit and are having a cold, cheap beer—PBR no doubt—at my expense, at some no-name, hole-in-the-wall bar. Getting a good laugh about how they pulled another one over on the city folk."

She swerved to miss a crater-sized pothole. The little car wobbled in protest, but she didn't let her foot off the gas pedal.

"Or they lured me out here to kill me and leave my body in small bits all down the countryside. Wasn't the Unabomber from Montana?"

Her cell phone chimed. "Great, we're back in range." Claire grumbled. The car didn't respond but kept pushing down the road. She had heard that phone coverage was sketchy at best in the wilderness, but she was going to a ranch. Surely a wide-open ranch range would have cell coverage.

Claire practically jumped out of her skin when her ringtone, Ed Sheeran's *Galway Girl,* filled the rental car in crescendo. "For heaven's sake!" she exclaimed as she reached for the phone that was sitting in one of the car's cup holders. She punched the phone icon and then put the call on speaker.

"Darling!" It was the melodious voice of her best friend. "Are you there? Is it as beautiful as everyone says? Are there lots of shirtless cowboys banging down your door, looking to bang you?"

Claire burst into laughter, despite herself. Grace had always been able to get her to laugh, no matter the circumstances. She was the Ying to Claire's Yang, which is why they made such a kick-ass writer/editor team.

"No. No men. Sorry to disappoint you," Claire apologized, knowing her voice sounded sweet and sour at the same time.

"What? That can't be true," Grace countered. "Have you at least seen some yummy ones?"

"Actually, I haven't seen a soul in more than an hour. Save for that furry thing I almost hit."

"You fly out to Montana, and suddenly you are an animal killer? For shame, Claire."

Claire laughed, despite the chastisement. "It ran out in front of the car. I think it was trying to kill me, whatever it was."

She had reached the main highway and swung the car around, determined to follow the directions to the letter.

"If you say so," Grace admonished. "But seriously, how is the cabin? Do you think you'll survive your writing holiday?" The way she said the words *writing holiday,* Claire knew Grace was making air quotes with her hands on the other end of the line.

"I haven't seen it yet. I don't even know where I am at this point. The directions I was given are completely useless. I've been driving the same stretch of road an hour. Everything looks the same. I'm supposed to be looking for some sort of turn off… but I haven't seen anything but grass. Grace? Grace? Are you there?" Claire glanced down at the cell phone when she didn't get an answer.

"Of course the call dropped. Why wouldn't the call drop? I'm in the middle of nowhere!" She slammed down on the brake pedal, just to emphasize her frustration to the poor rental car. It lurched to a stop immediately and then waited silently for its driver's next move.

Claire looked around, her head swiveling this way and that. All she saw was grass blowing in the wind, for miles and miles and miles all around. The words *empty prairie* come to mind, she thought. But then she caught a glimpse of what could have been considered a dirt road a few yards behind her. She threw the car in reverse and slowly backed up to it as if it might disappear if she approached it too fast. She eyed the road with all the suspicion of a distrustful detective and snatched the directions from the passenger seat. Her eyes quickly scanned the document then the landscape. Far off in the distance, she thought she could make out a building of some sort.

Suddenly she thrust the paper in the air and cried, "Victory!"

A flock of birds chose that exact moment to take flight from the bush, scaring the hell out of her. Claire screamed and then narrowed her eyes as she watched them grow small in the distance. But she was not to be deterred. Her small victory tasted too sweet. She quickly threw the car in drive and whipped onto the dirt road. Maybe this adventure wouldn't turn out so bad after all. One can only hope, she told herself.

* * *

Patrick Cole had watched the tiny car come up and down the main road a few times now and each time had gone back to tightening the fence line he was bent over. It was one of those "Smart-cars." He never did understand what was so smart about them. Around these parts, they joked that if you hit a squirrel, let alone a deer or even a raccoon, you would probably die. Everyone always got a good laugh out of that joke, and he figured it was just about true. Smart car indeed. Smart not to drive one in this country, more like.

Cole suspected the car's driver was his new guest. The only place he knew to rent such a vehicle was the Missoula airport; he didn't think they had them up in Kalispell yet. Yes siree. That little annoying thing zipping around like a lunatic had to be searching for his ranch. He was already beginning to regret the decision to rent out the small cabin, and it hadn't even started yet.

It had all been Julie's idea. But to no one's surprise, she was nowhere to be found now, and all the responsibility fell on his shoulders. Par for the course, really.

Foolish, that was what he had been. But the ranch needed the income. And now that his guest was here, he supposed he couldn't turn her away. But then again, if the little Smart-car and its driver never found the driveway, he couldn't exactly be held responsible for that, could he?

The Smart-car went cruising past his drive again. Cole couldn't help but let loose a small chuckle. He thought he had given pretty clear directions to Paradise Valley Ranch. Turn off the main highway three-quarters a mile past marker 136, ten miles after the turnoff and past the boulder that looked like a buffalo, turn on the dirt road, and follow that up to the main house. It was all pretty straightforward as far as he was concerned.

Just then, the car braked hard and skidded to a stop. Buck raised his head quickly from the gopher hole he had been vigorously investigating. The blue heeler cocked his head at Cole.

"I have no idea, buddy," Cole answered the silent question, shaking his head in wonder. "I have no idea."

The dog stuck his nose back to the ground, apparently

deciding the Smart-car excitement did not take precedence over gopher holes. Cole figured the dog had the right idea and went back to the fence line, though he couldn't help but notice when the car shifted into reverse and jolted back to the front of his driveway.

He grunted in amusement as the tiny car whipped itself onto the drive and began to barrel its way toward the main house. This was surely going to be some kind of adventure. Or some giant pain in the ass. Probably the latter, Cole decided. Buck yipped his agreement as he furiously dug into the soil, mud flying all around him.

"Next time I'm going to leave you out in the rain storm," Cole threatened the dog good naturedly. "I'm getting tired of bathing you all the time."

Just then, a high pitched whining sound filled the open air. Buck and Cole both jerked their heads up at the same time. Cole didn't realize what it was until he saw the tiny car jerking toward a puddle. It was a mud puddle that stretched almost across the entirety of his driveway. He barked out a harsh laugh before he could stop himself.

"Most people have sense enough to drive around a puddle that size," he told the dog, who was also watching the car's progress with keen attention.

Sure enough, the car made it almost exactly halfway through the puddle, then slowed, and then it sunk to a stop. It sat, quiet for a moment, and then the driver must have pushed the gas pedal down hard because the little tires started spinning as if their lives depended on it. Then the brake lights lit up, and the tiny car jerked, but it definitely hadn't made any progress toward dry land.

Buck snorted. The cycle repeated itself two or three times,

while Cole and his dog stood watching the spectacle. You'd have to pay good money in the city to see a routine like this, Cole thought, more amused than he probably should have been, given that he was about to be hosting this mess.

Finally, Cole sighed and started gathering up his tools. "Best go pull that car out," he told the dog. "It's only gonna sink deeper doing that. Foolhardy city folk… don't know nothing about nothing."

He finished loading the tools onto the four-wheeler and then climbed on. He started the old purring beast in one kick. Maybe it was going to be a lucky day after all because that certainly never happened. Cole was always telling the old piece of machinery that he was going to replace it, which only seemed to make it refuse to turn over with more and more frequency.

Buck was studiously ignoring Cole and frantically digging at a hole, desperate to get at something buried deep inside. Cole waited for half a second, and when the dog didn't budge, he whistled, sharp and short. The blue heeler took off at a dead run and then launched himself onto the back of the four-wheeler. He looked up at Cole with a load of false innocence in his eyes, his tongue was hanging out of his happy, grinning face.

Cole rolled his eyes but couldn't keep himself from rubbing the dog's head and scratching behind its ears. Damn dog had him wrapped around his paw, that was for certain sure. Cole huffed a laugh at the pup and then shifted the four-wheeler out of neutral and into first gear.

"Best go rescue the damsel in distress," he told the dog and hit the gas. After a moment of consideration, he added, "And her tiny, useless car."

2. The City Slicker and The Cowboy

Claire sat in the little car, cursing it with language that would have made her mother blush, and banging her hands against the steering wheel in a tantrum fit for an eight-year-old that was not allowed to eat an entire bag of cotton candy at a parade. When she was finished, she sat in silence. She could feel the car mocking her. Her face curled into a sneer.

Stupid car. What did it know! Claire Montague was a fierce woman with a smart head on her shoulders. She certainly wasn't going to let a little set back like this get under her skin or scare her back to the city.

Claire looked around her. All she could see were miles and miles of rolling plains, tall grass, and mountains in the distance. No help to be seen anywhere.

"Buck up buttercup," she told herself. "You are going to figure out how to get yourself out of this. No white knight in shining armor is going to ride up and rescue you. Lancelot and King Arthur are long gone."

Which was just fine, anyway. Claire had always despised that whole "white knight" idea. The girl was always staring up at the man with unconditionally adoring eyes, for one thing. And the man staring down at the girl like she was a rare truffle to be consumed with care, but consumed all the same. That kind of behavior reeked of Stockholm Syndrome. No, Claire was far too independent for that garbage. And as an independent, strong woman, she was going to get herself out of this mess.

She cautiously opened the door. The puddle she had driven into was threateningly close to spilling into the car. She groaned as she tried to recall the rental insurance. Could flooding possibly be one of the "accidents" it would cover? Or did they just assume any kind of flooding would sweep the little vehicle away and out to the open sea? Perhaps the car seat could be used as a flotation device.

"Enough dilly-dallying. Face the music, Claire," she grumbled to herself, while still eying the water line against the open car door. Carefully, she swung her feet out of the car and gingerly stepped into the murky depths.

Her heeled boots sunk into the mud further than Claire would have thought possible, and she threw her arm out against the top of the car to steady herself. She looked down. The designer boots came to her mid-calf and matched her knee-length skirt perfectly. And now there was muddy water threatening to slink down into the skin-tight boots as she wobbled, trying to shift her weight and gain some sort of balance.

What kind of backwoods land had she come to?

"Romantic country my ass," Claire muttered to the puddle, meaning every single syllable with all her heart, plus some.

She carefully closed the car door, hoping to prevent any flooding, and attempted to move out of the massive puddle. She needed to assess the damage before she could even begin to come up with a plan to get herself out of this mess. The mud sucked at her boots as she wadded through the water, almost falling and losing her balance the whole way to the edge of the blessed dry land.

Claire kept the stupid "Smart" car at her back as she put her hands on her hips and heaved in a few deep breathes. She might need to consider taking leg day at the gym more seriously if she got that winded from mud and water.

The air around her was utterly silent, save for her ragged breathing. Being from the city, she found it extremely eerie. Her internal apprehension started setting off alarm bells in the back of her mind. But then, almost as if her ears were adjusting to this new environment, she began to hear the birds calling to one another, the slight breeze fluttering flirtatiously with the grass lining the edges of the road, the buzz of one kind of bug or another. She closed her eyes and let it fill her senses.

Maybe this trip was exactly what she needed after all. If only she could figure out how the hell to get her rental car out of the crater it was currently drowning in. Claire huffed in determination and turned back around, facing her problem head-on. The car was still waiting for her, ever so patiently.

Claire circled the puddle. From what she could tell, the driver's side looked slightly more sunken in than the passenger's side. The puddle also seemed to be narrower on that side. Perhaps, if she could get some purchase, the car would pull itself out, just like trying to get a car unstuck after a snowstorm. It couldn't be that different, after all. Nature was nature.

The water sloshed against her legs, under her skirt, and dribbled into her boots as she slogged her way back to the car. She was far less careful than she had been trying to get out of the puddle. Claire was on a mission, and her clothes could be damned. It wasn't her best outfit anyway. And clearly, there was no one out here to look good for.

She jerked the driver's door open, causing a small wave and subsequent ripple throughout the muddy water. It hungrily lapped at the bottom of the car and slipped inside with little licks, pooling under the gas and brake pedals.

Claire had packed two suitcases for this trip, and at the airport, she had put them side by side in the back of the car. They had taken up the entire small space. She planned to get both of them on the passenger's side of the vehicle, giving it more weight and therefore solving her mud-crater dilemma. The car would then be able to ease itself out of the puddle, using the extra weight to gain purchase on the mud. And then all would be right in the world again. Well, except that her boots were now full of muddy water.

Instead of opening the hatchback, which could very well result in flooding the car altogether, Claire decided her best course of action was to pull the suitcase from behind the driver's seat into the passenger's seat. It had played out easier in her mind than it turned out to be in real life.

Not only was the suitcase too large to be easily handled, but it also didn't fit between the Smart-car bucket seats. Nor did it seem particularly inclined to be dragged out of its resting place. Claire wrestled with it longer than she probably should have before she gave up and decided she would have to open the hatchback and risk flooding. There was simply no other choice.

She shoved the suitcase back behind the driver's seat and climbed out of the car. She slammed the door in frustration and started to stomp her way around to the back of the car, until one of her boots seemed to get sucked down, immovably, into the mud. Her arms windmilled as she tried to keep her balance.

"No!" Claire cried out to the open sky as she went down. And then she was on all fours, half buried in muddy, slimy water. She brought her hands up and punched at the water, screaming in frustration. Brown water splashed up over every inch of her that wasn't already covered.

A rumbling sound filled the air when Claire's fit died out. She looked up and found an old truck cresting the small hill a dozen yards away. It was headed straight toward her and her catastrophe. And damned if that truck wasn't white.

* * *

When Cole and Buck arrived on the scene, the woman was dripping wet and covered in mud. The car hadn't moved, not even the smallest inch.

"How in the hell..." Cole let the unfinished question hang in the air of the truck cab. He slowly edged the truck toward the puddle, shifted into first gear, set the emergency brake, and turned the old beast off. "You'd better stay here, buddy," Cole reached over and scratched Buck's head in apology. "Lord only knows how a woman that got a car so stuck feels about dogs. She might not have a lick of common sense."

Buck yipped in disgruntlement but stayed where he was as Cole got out of the truck and slammed the door behind him.

It took restraint not to laugh as he studied the woman. Her long hair was soaked and dripping. Her clothes, which probably cost more than his whole wardrobe combined, were filthy. She looked like a spring calf who had been rolling in a field for the sheer pleasure of it, except for those eyes. Her lovely, big hazel eyes were boring into him with a fiery anger he doubted he had ever seen the likes of.

He tried to lighten the mood as he stood surveying the scene before him. "Most folks drive around the pond."

It didn't work. The woman's eyes narrowed, and it felt like an electric charge was crackling between them. Cole scuffed his work boots against the dirt driveway and found himself looking down. Damn, her eyes were lovely. And dangerous. He took a deep breath and tried again, raising his head to study the tiny car.

"Name's Patrick Cole," he introduced himself, keeping a serious look on his face. "Most of the folks around here just call me Cole. Patrick was my daddy's name. Calling me Cole caused less confusion for everyone."

The woman did not respond, didn't so much as blink, but she sure continued to glare at him. He caught a glimpse of her fists tightening out of the corner of his eye. For heaven's sake, it wasn't like he had put the puddle there for her to drive into. Cole heaved a sigh, turned around and started walking back to his truck.

The woman's voice cut through the air, sharp and on the edge of panic. "Where do you think you're going? You can't just leave me here!"

Cole opened the truck door, smiling at the old truck's familiar sound. Buck grinned at him as if he knew the woman was already getting under Cole's skin.

"Shut up," Cole refuted the dog's unspoken words. He pulled the bench seat forward and grabbed a tow rope from its hiding place.

"You can't leave me stranded." The woman's voice had moved into full panic mode.

Fool woman, he thought as he pushed his ball cap back and scratched at his forehead. Buck yipped. He wanted out of the truck. Cole just sighed and backed his way out of the cab and slammed the truck door shut. He held up the tow rope and waggled it to show the woman that he wasn't abandoning her to the fate of drowning in a mud puddle, though Cole didn't quite know why that idea amused him. He shook his head at himself and waded into the mud puddle.

"Oh." The woman's voice quietly reached his ears as he bent down and tried to find someplace to hook the tow rope onto the tiny car.

"I thought you were going to leave me out here," she said.

Maybe she meant it by way of apology, maybe not. Either way, it wasn't like he could leave her out here to fend for herself. Anyone without the sense to drive around a puddle wouldn't survive in this country for long without help. The land was a wild, untamable thing. And Cole loved every inch of it.

After a few minutes of searching for something substantial under the car to hook onto, he found some flimsy plastic part that he hoped would hold and set the tow rope. He stood slowly and risked a glance at the woman. Her eyes were less fiery than they had been, but no less lovely.

"We are a little different than city people around here," he drawled. When she raised her eyebrows in an unspoken question, he decided to explain. "We don't leave neighbors stranded to face their problems alone. That includes strangers, I suppose."

He didn't wait to hear her response but began to slosh his way out of the puddle, back toward his truck. The muddy water had filled his boots, and he knew it was going to take at least a day for them to dry out. He sighed again. Well, it was what it was.

It couldn't be helped.

Cole turned back to the woman. She hadn't moved from where she stood in the middle of the puddle, a few feet from the car. "Can you start that thing and put in it in drive?" After a few seconds, he added, "Please."

"Of course I can," she said defensively, splashing to the car door. "I'm not an idiot."

Cole just nodded his head. He hadn't been trying to imply anything; he just needed the car in drive.

"Don't push on the gas," he commanded. "I'm going to pull you out and then stop to unhook."

She shot him a glance hot enough to start a forest fire with wet wood. Cole tried to hide his smile as she struggled through the mud. Quite the little firecracker he had rented to. Yes, sir, it was going to be a long couple weeks of getting this woman out of scraps she should have been able to stay out of in the first place.

He hooked the tow rope onto the solid hook on the front of his truck and muttered something about real vehicles actually being useful. He glanced back at the puddle as he walked around to his driver's door. He really had no idea how the woman had gotten so stuck. Buck greeted him with a big dog tongue licking at his face. "Get off me," Cole chuckled as he pushed Buck back to the passenger side of the bench seat. "We've got a real... strong woman on our hands."

That woman had made it into her car, and Cole waved out his window, giving her a thumbs up. She gave him a thumbs up back through her windshield. And then she raised her hands away from her steering wheel as if to prove that she wasn't doing anything that he hadn't told her to.

"A real firecracker," Cole confided in Buck, who just continued to grin at him.

Cole shifted the truck in reverse and eased his water-filled boot onto the gas pedal, slowly starting to pull the car and the woman from the mud puddle. The truck purred, easily up to the task. Cole hmphed at the tiny car. Who drove those things, especially out here in the semi-wilderness? Tourists. That was the only answer. City tourists.

He pulled the car a few feet from the puddle and signaled for the woman to put her car in park. Cole unhooked the tow rope from both vehicles and walked to the driver's side of the car. The woman rolled down her window.

"Thank you," she said quietly, not looking him full in the face.

Cole nodded politely, touching the brim of his hat before saying, "You can follow me up to the house. We'll pull up to the cabin you're renting."

He was about to turn away when the woman thrust her hand out of the car window. "I'm Claire Montague."

Cole smiled and shook her hand. "I know."

He turned and began to walk back to the truck. He couldn't resist throwing one last comment over his shoulder, "Shouldn't be any more puddles for you to get stuck in. But you had better watch out just in case."

Cole was rewarded with the sound of a palm hitting a steering wheel and the whispered muttering of unladylike words. He couldn't help but chuckle and smile as he climbed into his old, white work truck.

3. The Deadline

Cole made sure to keep the truck puttering down the driveway at a dismal speed of ten and fifteen miles per hour. He didn't want to chance that the ridiculous little car couldn't keep up. He huffed at the whole absurd situation. He could only imagine what was going through the woman's head. Maybe she would do them both a favor and cut her stay short; there would be a partial refund, of course, and it would be worth it. He didn't need this kind of nonsense.

Buck happily yipped and practically vaulted over Cole as they pulled up to the guest cabin. The dog was off and running as soon as the truck door opened, chasing some phantom prairie dog, no doubt.

"Great," Cole muttered under his breath. "Now I have to face the dragon-lady tourist alone." He meant it in a joking way, sort of, but at the same time, there was some small grain of truth to it.

The woman pulled up and parked her car next to the truck, in front of the hitching post that sat at the front of the guest cabin.

An old relic from a different time. Cole had never seen the point of getting rid of it; it belonged here. The woman, however, was eying it with a look of distrust, or maybe that was just all the mud. Either way, she stayed seated in the car, glancing this way and that. What was she looking for? A shopping mall?

Cole glanced around the ranch yard. He loved this place, more than he was willing to admit to most folks. Letting an outsider in, well, it felt wrong somehow. But desperate times called for desperate measures, he supposed. Nothing to be done about it now.

He glanced back at the car as he heard the door open. The poor, sopping woman crawled from her refuge into the vast Big Sky countryside. She looked like a half-drowned raccoon.

"Welcome to Paradise Valley Ranch," Cole said with more than a little pride. He tried to smile and look welcoming like a good ranch host should. Claire stared him down with big eyes that narrowed just the slightest bit at his announcement. She was a drowned raccoon that could bite, then. Lovely.

"I might like it better once I'm not wearing half of it." She irritatingly gestured to the mud that covered her from head to toe, as if he might have been too simple to notice.

"Uh, yeah." Cole tried not to lose his host smile, but the words stung. How could someone ignore the beauty of the land? And on such a warm sunny day? Perhaps, the woman was a touch crazy in the head. It seemed like a good idea to get her settled and then hightail it out of there before anything else could go wrong. "Here is where you'll be staying."

He led her to the front porch of the cabin and opened the door, gesturing for her to enter. The cabin itself had been updated with a kitchenette, half bath, and pillow-top queen-size bed. It wasn't grand, but then, he had never intended to rent it out, let alone be a five-star resort.

"Quaint," Claire said, standing just outside the doorway.

Was that a hint of sarcasm in her voice? Cole gritted his teeth and tried to keep the city woman from getting under his skin. At this rate, two weeks was going to feel like a long ten years.

"My great-grandfather built it for my great-grandmother. She said she needed a place that had some peace and quiet, where she could look at the mountains and the big open sky. Back then everyone, ranch hands included, stayed in the big house. It's not a wonder that she wanted a small spot where she could feel the call of the land," Cole smiled as he recited the cabin history from memory. It was something that had been passed down from generation to generation.

The tourist's face was unamused. Cole decided he needed to cut the story short and get on with it already. This guest-ranch deal was already proving to be more trouble than it was worth.

"It's updated now. As modern as I can make it. There is a back porch through there." He gestured toward a back door on the other side of the one-room cabin. "Julie put up those pictures and what not. This whole renting the cabin was her idea. I hope it's homey for you."

Cole wanted to bite his own tongue off. He had never been so chatty in his life! Friends had told him, more than once, that he was the stoic, silent type. And for the most part, he agreed. Maybe a whole winter cooped up indoors had gotten to him this year. Damn blizzards.

Claire had been nodding her head, but Cole could tell she wasn't really interested in his rambling. Frankly, he wasn't either. It was definitely time to hightail it out of there. Evening was upon the ranch. The sun was beginning to dip behind the mountains, casting the long shadows of evening over the yard.

There were things that had to be done yet before the day was over.

"I'll get your luggage and leave you to it, then." Cole turned to make a quick exit.

"You don't have to do that," Claire said suddenly, putting her hand on his arm as he passed.

"It's all part of the hospitality package, ma'am." He looked straight into her eyes and tipped his hat. He could have sworn he caught a small smile playing on her lips. His heart skipped a beat at that, though he would deny it nine ways to Sunday should anyone happen to ask. Patrick Cole was not one to become infatuated with a pretty smile. I must not have had enough water today, he thought to himself as he cleared the door frame, half shaking his head.

A moment later he was opening the hatchback of the tourist's tiny car, marveling that she had fit the two huge suitcases into such a small space. He tugged the monstrosities out of the car and was surprised at their weight. How many sets of clothes did you need for a two-week stay?

He glanced toward the cabin and caught a glimpse of his guest over the top of the car roof. She was bent over, trying to tug off her ruined, fancy boots on the front porch. She pulled with a force that almost knocked her over. Water and mud came gushing out as her foot yanked free. Cole almost laughed aloud but caught himself in time. The poor woman had had enough embarrassment for one day. And as a city slicker in his valley, there was surely more to come in the next two weeks.

* * *

Claire slept later than she had meant to. In fact, she could feel the full force of the sun on her face before she even opened her eyes. She stretched out her limbs and groaned with the pleasure of waking up when one's body wanted to, instead of when an alarm demanded it. That is what a vacation was all about. But she was here to write, not to vacation, much to her chagrin.

Groaning again, she opened her eyes slowly, only to see a massive artistic print of a buffalo staring down at her from the opposite wall. Her body jerked in surprise and then relaxed and then tensed again as she remembered how eventful her adventure had been the previous day.

Yet another groan filled the room as Claire threw an arm over her eyes, trying to block out the memories of her disastrous arrival to her new, temporary home. Her new home for the next two weeks, that is. She couldn't have been more embarrassed. The bright side was that it would make a good story at the next dinner party she attended. It was complete with a villain and all! Hell, that wretched man had probably hopped right down to a local hole-in-the-wall bar to regale the whole room with stories of his new guest. Claire was willing to bet her next advance that there were horses tied up in front of that bar instead of cars. This was Big Sky Country after all. She snorted at the mental picture.

Yesterday, she couldn't wait for him to leave her alone. She had wanted sleep and solitude, but she hadn't realized how quiet it would be. Without the sounds of the city – cars, buses, people and their sweater-wearing dogs – Claire had felt an utter stillness inside of her that she wasn't entirely comfortable with. In the end, she had played some tunes off her phone at full volume while she showered and washed the mud puddle off into a distant, fading memory.

Claire groaned again and forced herself to sit up in the

comfortable bed. Though she would be happy to stay in bed all day, there was a coffee pot across the room, and it was calling her name. It was the sole reason she could convince herself to throw the covers back and swing her legs over the side of the bed. She stepped on something hard and pointy and fell back on the bed, crying out in pain.

She bent down and picked up her travel alarm clock. She knew she had set it the night before! She must have pulled another Claire Montague Special and thrown it when it had sounded its hideous ringing. This had happened before, more than once, and Claire had learned that she needed to buy the sturdiest alarm clocks money could afford. Which more often than not meant the tiny fold-up ones from Walmart – oddly enough. Sleep had always held a strong grip on her life. Apparently, Montana wasn't going to change that.

Coffee, her foggy mind started chanting, slowly getting louder and louder. Yes, she needed coffee. Lots and lots of coffee. She stumbled over to the coffee maker and dumped some delicious smelling grounds, provided with the coffee maker, in the basket without measuring. The stronger the brew, this morning anyway, the better. Claire held the bag to her nose and inhaled a deep breath. The bag was labeled Montana Coffee Traders, Grizzly Blend. Claire made a mental note to pick some up to take home with her as she huffed the bag again.

As the coffee pot began to gurgle, she went about brushing her teeth and washing her face. She may have been in the wilderness, but that would be no excuse if her face were to break out, or if her breath were to become comparable to a grizzly bear's. She chuckled at herself, enjoying the mental picture her wit provided for the comparison. This is why she was an author. Her mind was quick on its feet with words, and somehow her hands were able to convey that by typing hundreds of thousands of words over the years.

"On that note," she said aloud to the gurgling coffee pot. "Time to get cracking."

She poured a cup of steaming coffee into a camp-style, large, speckled mug, and walked out onto the back porch of the cabin – because procrastination. What she saw stunned her. The mountains, they were majestic. Truly majestic. How she had missed their breathtaking power when she arrived the day before, she had no idea. Well, probably because she'd been covered in mud and irritated by a dumb cowboy. But still. She could easily lose herself in their beauty forever. As if on cue, her cell phone started to ring from inside the cabin.

Claire sucked down a gulp of hot coffee, sufficiently burning her tongue, and hurried inside to catch the call. She picked it up just before it switched over to voicemail, but she only heard scratches and bits of a voice on the other end of the line. Great, cell service was going to be awesome here. Just her luck. She held the phone away from her ear to glance at the caller ID. It was her editor. Damn. She really needed to take this.

"Hold on, Grace!" Claire shouted into the phone, and she sloshed the coffee cup down onto her nightstand. "I don't have great service."

The answer on the other end of the line didn't even sound like a human language.

"Damn it!" Claire cursed the countryside and all its splendor, again. It was not making her life easier like it was supposed to. That had been the whole point of coming out to this godforsaken cabin in the first place!

Eventually, she ended up huddled in the front-right corner of the cabin behind a small wood stove. She was standing on her tip toes and had her head angled as high up as she could manage.

"Grace?" she asked wearily, thoroughly stressed. "Can you hear me?"

"Can you hear me now." Grace's voice came through loud and clear, without any hint of amusement at her own joke. In fact, it didn't even sound like a question, like it was meant to on all those commercials.

"Hi, Grace," Claire said with a smile her editor couldn't see. "Sorry about that."

"You must really be in the middle of nowhere. Are you sure you will survive?"

"To be honest, I very well may not," Claire answered truthfully and then launched into her tale of misery from the day before. By the end, Grace sounded like she had fallen on the floor and was close to peeing her pants.

"It's not that funny," Claire was trying not to let her own amusement bleed into her voice. She bit her lip to contain her grin.

"I've always said you have a flair for the dramatic. It's what makes you a New York Times Bestseller," Grace commented between gasps for air. "But I have never heard the likes of that story before. God in heaven above!" She burst into another fit of laughter.

"Yeah, yeah, yeah." Claire didn't really think she was that dramatic, but it was a good story.

"So…" Grace tried to switch gears, even as she still sounded like she was having trouble stifling the laughter. "How is the manuscript coming?"

"I only just arrived, you know. But I got a little work done this morning," Claire lied. This was how the relationship with her editor and long-time friend worked. She lied about getting things done and then did her best work right before the deadline. It had proved a successful formula for them both, and Grace hadn't been the wiser. Yet.

"See!" Grace crowed triumphantly. "I told you a writing retreat would work for you. And you were worried because you had never been on one before." A scoff huffed out of the phone and met Claire's ear as she rolled her eyes. Good thing she wasn't face to face with her friend.

"Sure, sure," she pretended to admit and glanced at her laptop case.

"That deadline won't even be an issue now that you are cranking it out. I'll have to send an update to the big wigs."

Claire could hear Grace's fingers flying across her keyboard even as she said the words. Awesome.

"Hold on now," Claire attempted to caution her editor. "Whatever I write could be really terrible. Don't count our chickens yet. Please, Grace."

Grace huffed. "Yeah, right."

Claire rolled her eyes. She was going to have to produce something special to keep the publishing company off her back this time. She was six months overdue on this manuscript, something she had never done before. In fact, she had always prided herself on not being one of "those authors."

Only then did Claire realize her toes and calves were starting to cramp from trying to stay perfectly still in the good cell-service spot.

"Listen, Grace. I'd better go. I need to drink some more coffee and get cracking."

"Sure, sure," Grace murmured. Claire could almost see her, proofreading her own email and only half listening. "There!

Sent."

Claire inwardly groaned. Awesome, she thought. Just... Awesome.

"There is one more thing." Claire did not like the tone Grace's voice took on. "I heard from Chad."

A bottomless pit opened inside of Claire. Her stomach dropped obediently and kept tumbling over and over and over. She couldn't form words.

"I know it ended badly with you two. And I'm sorry to bring it up," Grace's words poured out of the phone in a rush. "He wouldn't leave me alone until I promised to say something to you."

Claire still couldn't summon words. And for a writer, that was a genuinely terrible feeling.

"He says he is sorry. And that he wants to give it another go."

"I have to go." Claire didn't wait for a response before hanging up, wandering over to the bed, crumbling to the floor. She sat there stunned for several minutes before picking herself up and slogging back over to the coffee maker.

"Buck up, girl," she told herself. "You have a book to write. And that asshole isn't going to stop you."

She emptied the rest of the coffee pot into her mug and set about making another batch. The poor little machine would have to work overtime today. Claire straightened her shoulders and went for her laptop case.

4. The Ranch

Cole had woken with the sun that morning, as he did every morning. A life of ranch work had enabled him to ditch alarm clocks years ago. His body woke after it got enough sleep and he was always ready to face the day. Except for maybe this day. He found himself finding extra, little meaningless jobs to do around the ranch and drinking extra coffee, before he finally got in his truck and headed toward the main highway.

He wished he was able to bring Buck with him. The dog could always bring a smile to his face. However, banks tended to frown upon four-legged friends in their establishments. Even out here in Big Sky Country.

Damn, he really didn't want to face this day.

Cole glanced at the guest cabin as he rolled out of the ranch yard. All was quiet. The tiny car sat silently, covered in mud, just where the woman had parked it the evening before. Claire, Cole reminded himself. The woman's name was Claire. A faint smile lit his face as he remembered what she had looked like standing in that giant mud puddle. Fool city folk, he thought to himself as he chuckled.

As he watched the guest cabin fade in his review mirror, he reset his mouth into a stern line. He needed to focus. He had a case to make. And he would need every ounce of negotiating power he could muster.

"I could really use your help today," he threw out a prayer to his ancestors, who had all ranched the land before him. Maybe their wisdom and divine intervention would see a way out of this mess that he couldn't. It was a long, silent, foreboding ride into town.

* * *

"Howdy, Cole." Bob Foster aggressively pumped Cole's arm in greeting, his jowls shaking with the effort. "Good to see you. Good to see you."

"Yes, sir," Cole replied, half trying to pull his arm back. He didn't want to give offense, but he didn't want his arm to be plied off either. "Good morning to you, Mr. Foster."

"Bob, my boy," Mr. Foster replied, finally letting go of the death-grip handshake. "Call me Bob. It's what your grand-pappy called me. Your daddy too."

"Yes, sir." Cole cleared his throat. The last thing he wanted to talk about was his father or how he had called this overlord "Bob."

"Let's go to my office, son." Mr. Foster, Bob, led Cole to the back of the small bank. His back was slightly stooped, though not enough that he needed a cane. The man wore cowboy boots and Levis that hadn't and never would see a day of honest work. His blazer was a deep gray. It gracefully covered his pressed white shirt and emphasized his turquoise bolo tie. The giant turquoise rock was probably real and worth more than Cole's whole wardrobe. Cole caught a glimpse of the eagle that graced the rock as Bob held the office door open with one hand and ushered him forward with the other.

The man prided himself on his sense of patriotism, which is why his office sported an old cavalry American flag and a painting of white cowboy buffalo hunters. There was also a mounted set of Texas Longhorns. Cole was sure all of the pomp impressed some people. But not him. He had much more respect for those who had calloused hands of hard work than the soft hands of someone who just told glory stories from years when buffalo were killed in the thousands, and Native Americans were being driven to their deaths through starvation and the reservation system. But he had to play nice today.

"Have a seat, have a seat right there," Mr. Foster said as he closed his office door and tilted his head.

"Thank you kindly," Cole replied and sat in one of the small office chairs across from the bank president's massive oak desk. Play nice, he told himself, play nice.

"So," Mr. Foster said with a sigh, as he lowered himself into a creaking leather office chair. "How is that pretty little valley of yours these days?"

Cole choked back a sneer at the predatory glint that alighted the old man's eyes. "Fine. Just fine. The fence held up great this winter. I'm finishing the last perimeter check."

"Heard you were taking on a guest."

Damn, news traveled fast. "Yes, sir. In my grandmother's cabin."

"You could turn that whole operation into a dude ranch and make buckets of money, you know."

"That's about the last thing I want to spend my days doing.

With all due respect, sir."

"Oh?" Mr. Foster cocked an eyebrow at Cole and leaned forward over his desk. Cole could only assume it was an attempt to make him feel like a foolish boy. The man had applied such tactics before.

"That's right. Catering to a bunch of tourists sounds like a special kind of hell." He looked down and studied his rough hands rather than continue to meet the banker's eye.

Mr. Foster burst into a hearty laugh that caused Cole's head to snap back up as he shifted uneasily in his seat. "You have that right, son," the old man said between bursts of chuckles. He shook his head, causing those jowls to sway above and against his shirt collar.

Cole hated that the man called him "son." He had been coming to this bank since he was a kid with his grandfather, and Mr. Foster didn't seem to want to let the habit die. Come to think of it, the man had looked about a hundred years old even back then. Maybe his money kept him alive. Or maybe it was the greed.

"Well, you are probably going to have to do something that you don't like, son. And real soon." Mr. Foster turned somber and serious without batting an eyelash. Cole was almost taken aback, but then reminded himself that Mr. Foster had been playing this game for a long, long time.

"You have foreclosed on six ranches in the last year. And every one of them is still for sale." Cole could play hardball too. "Every one of them is just sitting there, good land wasting away."

Mr. Foster leaned back, the leather chair creaking, and studied Cole. "I've dealt with your family for generations, Patrick."

"Cole would be just fine." Cole had had about all of the fake niceness he could stomach for the day. He might as well stop pretending; the banker already had. The old man's eyes turned into tiny hard bits of coal. Cole guessed his heart looked about the same.

"Now you listen here." Mr. Foster's voice had dropped an octave, and he leaned forward, resting his big, beefy hands on the desk. "Your granddaddy did a good job with that land. Always turned a profit. But your daddy..." Mr. Foster let the words hang in the air too long, much too long for Cole's taste. "Well, we all know the story. Your daddy took that loan out against the land and then up and disappeared."

It didn't matter how many times people brought it up, that little bit of history always felt like a punch in the gut. Cole kept his face a picture of calm, but his insides were roiling.

"It was a raw deal he cut," Mr. Foster continued. "I tried to tell him so. But he insisted."

Yeah, I bet you did, Cole thought to himself. You old, selfish bastard.

"Ran off with that woman." The man was trying to rub salt in an ancient, open wound. And it was working, but Cole refused to rise to the occasion. "You ever hear from him anymore?"

"No, Mr. Foster," Cole tried to hide the anger in his voice. "I haven't heard from that man since he walked out on my sixteenth birthday. Safe to say he won't be helping to pay back your loan."

Mr. Foster sighed and made a disgruntled sound. Cole hoped he was frustrated that his tactics were failing to get Cole all worked up.

"It isn't my loan. I was doing your family a favor by trying to talk him out of it!" Mr. Foster practically spit out the words.

"There isn't enough money in the cattle you raise. If you can't figure something else out, I'll be forced to call your loan into default at the end of next month."

The words took his breath away, but Cole had known they were coming. Yet, he still had to work hard not to show any kind of reaction in front of the banker. Cole was going to be the bigger, better man – just like his granddad had taught him. He didn't owe Mr. Foster a damn thing, but he did owe it to himself to do what was best for Paradise Valley.

"If you hadn't drained your savings account on God knows what," Mr. Foster's voice droned on. "We might have been able to work something out." The man leaned back into his office chair like he was ready to take Cole into his confidence and help him. If only Cole would lay himself bare, like a sacrificial lamb being led to slaughter. If only Cole would give up all his secrets. "What did you spend all that money on anyway?"

Cole took a deep breath to steady himself. "Frankly, it's none of your business." He had to work not to spit the words out. "Good day to you, Mr. Foster."

Before the banker could get another word in, Cole swiftly stood and strode from the office and out of the bank, tipping his hat politely to the teller on his way out.

It hadn't gone the way he had wanted it to, the way he had hoped it might. Hell, it hadn't gone the way he desperately needed it to go. But realistically, he didn't know what else he could have expected. His grandfather had been able to charm the bank into giving the ranch several extensions over the years. He had eventually paid off everything, securing the land for future generations. Or so he had thought. But Cole had never been able to charm the snake that was Mr. Foster, not like his granddad had been able to.

Cole's father had taken a mortgage out against the land and then mysteriously disappeared. Some folk said he went off in pursuit of a rodeo queen from North Dakota. The man had never had a hand for ranching. Maybe he had just gotten so sick of it, he sought to ruin it when he left. Or perhaps he thought that Cole's grandfather would be able to magically pay back the loan. Whatever the case, a year later, Cole had taken full responsibility for the ranch. His grandfather had taken ill and was dead before anything could be done about it.

And so every year, the payments Cole had been able to make got smaller and smaller. Mr. Foster was right about one thing, cattle did not pull in the money like they once did. Cole desperately wished his grandfather was still here to advise him. He had run out of ideas, and with Mr. Foster threatening to default the loan, hope was waning.

Cole climbed into his truck without a backward glance at the bank. He could feel Mr. Foster's little coal eyes fixed on him from a window, just like a villain from an old western before a shootout. Cole studiously ignored the open challenge and turned his truck over. He needed to go home. He needed to feel his little spit of land beneath his feet and breathe in the fresh mountain air. He needed to quell the dangerous combination of anger and despair rising in his body and spirit.

5. The Attraction

Claire sat with her back straight and her fingers hovering over her keyboard. The blinking cursor on the laptop screen seemed to be mocking her with its flashing persistence. Every few flashes of the damned cursor were interrupted with the blink of an image of Chad, provided by her stupid, stupid mind.

Flash, flash, blink. Flash, flash, blink.

She pushed her laptop away with more force than it deserved and ran her hand roughly through her hair, pausing to grip it when she hit a tangle. Claire fought the urge to scream in frustration, though no one would hear her out in the middle of nowhere. Six months, for six long months her life had consisted of this ridiculous mind game.

"Ack!" The half-shouted sound of frustration escaped out of her. She was known within publishing circles as a prolific writer. It meant she could pump out book after book after book without blinking an eyelash. And her readers ate it up. It was what made her money. And Claire loved it. She was good at it. That is, up until stupid Chad and that whole debacle.

Oh, how those readers and publishers would laugh if they could see her now. Tearing at her own hair, over a boy. A stupid boy! And Grace, dear Grace would think she was losing her mind. Claire was acting worse than some of the characters she had written, and that was kind of saying something.

"Damn it!" She let go of her hair and rubbed at her eyes. The whole point of coming out in the middle of nowhere was to escape thoughts of that wretched man. Coffee. Maybe she just needed more coffee. As if that poor little coffee pot hadn't been working in overdrive since the moment Claire had opened her eyes that morning.

She started yet another batch of the magical brew in the tiny four-cup pot. Was this number three or four for the day? Claire tended to lose count. Not that she cared. The more coffee, the better. Even more so if Phantom Chad was going to live in her head and continually try to take over her life. He had never liked coffee. Well, if he was going to live up there, he had better get used to it.

Claire huffed in amusement at the idea of Phantom Chad getting upset over her coffee consumption. Maybe it would poison the blinking vision of his face. It would serve him right, too. The thought brought an evil grin to her lips. Yes, that idea made her feel better. Take that, blinking vision of Chad's face!

As she waited for the coffee to brew, Claire stretched out her limbs. They had gone stiff from sitting so long without any movement beyond hair pulling and lip biting. She took in a deep breath and was vaguely aware of the lack of city smell behind the aroma of coffee. Another deep breath filled her lungs, and she let it out slowly through her nose. The middle of nowhere, it may have been, but it was so peaceful she almost couldn't remember what a city smelled, sounded, or felt like. A true paradise this might be after all.

The quiet of the moment was disrupted by an odd thumping sound. Claire, with her body relaxed and Phantom Chad forgotten, couldn't place the sound. She was sure she had never heard anything like it. Was it a wild animal? Or a cow? There it was again! As the coffee gurgled and spit out the last dregs of its brew, Claire cautiously tried to peer around the curtains of her tiny cabin.

She didn't see anything that could possibly be making that sound. It was going to drive her mad. Well, it was better that than stupid Phantom Chad, she supposed. But still. She had to know what it was! Arming herself with a mug of coffee, she cautiously ventured out the front door of the cabin.

Claire was immediately greeted by a blue heeler bounding up to her and greeting her with his wet tongue. He seemed to be a very happy little fellow, content to bask in the attention she gave him. Claire had always loved dogs, and couldn't resist crouching down to give him a belly rub. But soon, a sharp whistle had the dog up and flying across the yard.

Claire stood and looked around the property in front of her cabin. There was the dirt driveway she had driven up yesterday. To the right of that road, there was a big barn. Though she would have guessed it would be red (because weren't all farm and ranch barns red?), the structure was actually a natural wood color. Probably stained with some weather-protecting stuff, if she had to guess. There was no doubt it had been taken care of over the years.

A corral was attached to the barn, just like in old western movies. No horses, though. A few dozen yards away from the barn-corral combo was a big ranch house.

It was impressive. The snow-capped mountains standing tall

behind it only served to enhance its beauty. Claire was sure that this was what billionaires modeled their vacation homes after. This was the genuine article. A wraparound porch graced the front of the house, complete with a rocking chair. She could tell it had high ceilings and, if she had to guess, she would say the second level was almost all bedrooms. Someone had done an outstanding job converting it from a ranch house to a modern-day home. That is if Patrick Cole's story was to be believed.

Speaking of which, the man himself strode out of the ranch house screen door and made his way toward the corral, Buck grinning at his heels. Claire's breath caught in her throat as her eyes involuntarily followed the lines of his muscular chest, arms, and back. That man could take off his shirt around her any day. Her face felt flushed, but she knew that had to be the result of her hot coffee. She forced herself to look away from the gorgeous man and at her coffee instead. Both her hands were holding the mug, and they were definitely not trembling.

The odd thumping sound started again, but sharper now, reminding Claire why she had come outside in the first place. She scanned the landscape in front of her, trying not to think about the man and his muscles. But of course, it was him making the noise.

It appeared that the man was chopping wood. Claire watched as he raised the ax above his head with both hands and brought it down onto a log, cleanly splitting it in two. Both pieces fell to either side of the chopping block. He gracefully stooped and set up one of the pieces for another go. It too cleanly split with the downward swing of his ax. It was like watching a work of art.

Admittedly, the only previous experience that Claire had with this type of thing was an episode of *The Bachelor*. Said bachelor was comically bad at chopping wood, but the women fawned over him nonetheless. Fools, every one of them. And yet, here she was, practically drooling.

There was that movie too, *The Proposal,* where Ryan Reynolds' character was hollowing out a canoe. But Claire didn't know if that actually counted as chopping wood. But the man had looked very, very good doing it. Even more so in the next scene when he and Sandra Bullock accidentally run into each other while naked. Clearly, she had watched the film more than once. Wood chopping, canoe hollowing – she could watch either one all day.

Well, the good news was that she knew exactly what the hero of her book was going to look like.

Claire took a big gulp of coffee with a blush in her cheeks. She had best go talk to the man instead of standing there all day, staring at him with googly eyes. Besides, the dog was there. And she liked that dog a lot.

* * *

Cole had set about getting to work as soon as he was back on the ranch. Something about the methodical practice of ranching had always set his soul at ease. It didn't hurt that he was thinking about Mr. Foster's head every time he brought the ax down into a new, soft piece of birch. Something about the man had always seemed so criminal to Cole. The interaction they had shared that day had not helped sway that opinion.

He was so focused on his work that he didn't notice his guest approaching until Buck jumped up and trotted happily over to the woman. Cole leaned the ax against the corral and reached for his shirt. He tried not to watch the woman from the corner of his eye as he shoved his arms through the sleeves.

"Hi," he said lamely as he turned, leaving the shirt unbuttoned. He removed his hat and used his hand to wipe at the sweat on his forehead. The woman was studiously ignoring him in favor of his dog, who was soaking up the attention like he had never been loved in all his long life. Traitor, Cole thought. Buck always did have a soft spot for the womenfolk.

Cole cleared his throat and tried again. "How is the cabin treating you?"

The woman stood but left a hand on Buck's furry head. The dog grinned at Cole as if to prove a point.

"I fear I've abused your poor little coffee pot today." The woman offered him a small smile. She was quite lovely when she wasn't covered in mud. Well, she had been lovely then too. And scary. Dragon scary.

"Yeah," Cole drawled, offering his own smile. "That can happen. I may have had a cup or two too many this morning as well."

They stood in awkward silence, neither seeming to know where to take the conversation. Both Cole and Claire caught each other stealing glances. Cole couldn't help but notice how her golden-brown hair caught the sunlight. Her mouth quirked and then she raised her eyebrow at him. Damn it, he'd been caught staring. Not cool.

"I'm sorry?" he attempted to recover.

"I asked what you were doing," Claire snickered and tossed her hair. She raised her coffee mug to take another sip while she waited patiently for his answer. Her mouth still held that perfect, adorable little smirk.

"Oh!" Cole looked back at the wood pile and shrugged.

"Ahh... just chopping wood. The nights can still be cold out here at the base of the mountains, even though its spring. Figured I'd make sure there was a good stock for the stoves."

Claire made a confirming noise and took another sip of coffee. Buck was still sitting politely at her feet.

"You are much better at it than The Bachelor," she commented.

"The Bachelor?" Cole pushed his hat back and wiped at the sweat that was continuing to gather there. He did not miss Claire's eyes traveling up and down his tall frame.

"Never mind," Claire murmured. She stood straighter and cleared her throat. "I did notice the wood stove in the cabin. I have no idea how to use it."

Cole chuckled. He hadn't considered having to give lessons on how to start a fire with the cabin rental. Though the thought of being close to Claire didn't bother him one bit. It was a good thing he hadn't rented to a hairy Sasquatch instead of the scary dragon-lady tourist.

"It's no problem. If it looks like we might get a cold spell, I'll take care of it."

"Thank you." Claire looked up at him through thick lashes. Then she cleared her throat and shifted on her feet.

Buck, without any kind of warning, took off at a dead sprint into a side field. Cole watched him go, merely for something to focus his attention on, ignoring the awkward silence and tension that seemed to be building.

"What the?" Claire half asked.

"Oh, he probably saw a prairie dog," Cole explained. "They have a bit of a private war going on."

"And you just let him take off like that? What's his name anyway? What if a bear came along?"

"Buck, his name is Buck. And there isn't much trouble he can get in. I bet he knows every gopher hole in the county by now."

"I suppose he might be better equipped than those little city dogs."

"That he is," Cole admitted, not trying to sound too proud. He'd raised Buck from a tiny, little sickly pup into the monster that he was.

"Well…" Claire sighed. "I'd best get back to work."

Cole nodded and started to turn back to his waiting ax.

"And thank you for," Claire paused, "informing me about the procedure of wood chopping."

She turned on her heel and walked quickly back across the ranch yard to her cabin. Cole stood watching her until she closed the cabin door. He couldn't force himself to look away. After the door closed, he shed his shirt and picked up his ax, mentally scolding himself the whole time.

What kind of host was he, checking out his guest and getting all flustered around her. He didn't have time for that kind of nonsense right now. Not when his life, his land, his whole livelihood was being threatened. He attacked the woodpile with more vigor and was vaguely aware of a pair of eyes watching him from the cabin.

6. The Dirt

The next morning, Claire managed to get up with her alarm rather than throwing it across the room like a zombie. She stretched and groaned, breathing in a deep lungful of pure Montana air. It smelled faintly of pine trees, but not the pine-tree candles everyone seemed to be so fond of at Christmas time. No. This was a real piney, woody, heady scent, and Claire thought she might love it.

After a few moments of contemplating candles and Christmas, without any unwanted thoughts of stupid Chad popping up, Claire forced herself out of bed and stumbled over to the coffee maker. She was slightly dismayed when she picked up the bag of coffee grounds and found that there were only enough roasted beans left for two or three pots. Claire could quickly go through that in a morning, especially with this little four-cup pot.

She sighed in dismay as she poured some of the precious beans into the filter. Perhaps it wouldn't be such a bad idea to go into town anyway. Claire could use some supplies, and Grace would get a kick out of a receiving a postcard from her wild travels. She started to make a mental checklist as she brushed her teeth and threw her hair into a single braid that curved down over her shoulder - her preferred, easy, go-to style.

The coffee pot gurgled loudly, signaling the end of it's brewing cycle. Claire poured a generous amount of the dark liquid into her mug and attempted to take sips in between dressing – pulling on a pair of jeans and shimming into a plain t-shirt. Plain Jane was the name of the game in this country. At least, that was what she had learned after her mud-puddle experience. Besides, it was more comfortable this way, and she didn't have anyone out here to impress, she told herself.

As if summoned by the very thought, an image of a sexy man chopping wood flashed, momentarily, through Claire's mind. It startled her so much, she almost dropped her mug of coffee, which was still half full. That kind of image had no business popping up! Sure, the cowboy was attractive. But he was also rude and quick to laugh at her "city-ness." See the mud-puddle incident as proof. The last thing she needed was a schoolgirl crush on the man. In fact, right in that very moment, Claire resolved to avoid Patrick Cole as much as possible over the next few days. She was here to do a job, and by God, she would get it done.

With the coffee mug still in hand, Claire found her way to the back porch of the cabin. She was hoping the fresh air would clear her head, clear out any confusion. The mountains indeed were breathtaking. Snow still crusted their peaks, while the lower halves were a curious mixture of blues and greens. It was picture perfect and more. Claire knew she would never be able to describe them in the way they deserved, not even on her best day of writing.

6. The Dirt

Buck came trotting around the corner and made a beeline for her, like he thought she was just there waiting on him. Claire couldn't help but smile. She liked the little heeler, and the happy little chap seemed to have taken a shine to her as well. Crouching down, she reached to scratch behind his ears, as he politely dropped a bright-green tennis ball at her feet.

"Oh ho!" Claire grinned at the dog. "Fancy a little fetch, do you?"

The dog grinned back and sat patiently while Claire tossed the ball into the air a couple of times, teasing the poor little guy. Then, quick as lightening, she launched the ball off into a distant field. She half jumped and gasped as some of the coffee sloshed out of the mug she was still holding.

Buck took off at a dead run and was back with the ball before Claire could dry her hand on her jeans. He dropped the drool-covered ball at her feet. Claire grinned down at him; his begging eyes were too much. She picked up the ball and relaunched it, laughing as the dog raced to it and pounced.

She had always wanted a dog, but city life wasn't quite as conducive to such luxuries. Nor did Claire fancy taking a dog out onto the side of her apartment building several times a day for the dog to "do its business." No, she would want to have a dog somewhere more like this – open space, long throws for the pup to fetch, enough fresh air for everyone. Not one dog sweater in sight.

Back and forth she and the dog went, several more times, before she noticed the cowboy standing off the side of her cabin. He seemed to be watching her with some interest, eyes alight with… something she couldn't place her finger on. She tried to tell herself he was only watching to make sure she, the crazy city lady, didn't steal his beloved dog. But even as she let those thoughts spin through her head, her stomach squeezed a little tighter. Traitor, she told it.

Claire stood straighter and tossed her braid over her shoulder, trying to give off an air of nonchalance. She threw the ball again for her new friend. Would serve you right, she silently told the cowboy, if Buck liked me more than you.

"You have a good arm." Cole's voice sounded like a rich cup of coffee. At least, that is how she would have described it if she were writing him as a character in one of her books. Get a grip, girl, Claire chided herself.

"I guess," she told Cole, while making sure her gaze was fixed on the dog. "I grew up playing streetball with the boys in the neighborhood. They didn't like it so much when I pitched better than they did."

Cole chuckled, a rich and warm sound. "I just bet they didn't. But Buck here, he sure seems to appreciate your arm."

Claire turned toward the man after launching the tennis ball to find him smiling at her. Genuinely smiling. Perhaps this was some sort of olive branch?

"Poor dog just thinks I neglect him all the time," Cole continued. "But he sure comes running fast enough when I fill his food bowl." Claire cocked her head and let a small smile grace her lips. She couldn't puzzle the man out.

"He does seem quite neglected," she agreed, hoping there wasn't too much amusement showing on her face. "Say, are there any coffee shops in town? I need to get some work done where this little fella isn't distracting me."

"Sure. There is only one that you would consider a real coffee shop. Morning Star's place. It's on main street. Kind of a gift shop, coffee, catch-all kind of place. But she has a couple of tables set up near the coffee bar, and the coffee itself is the best for miles around."

"Awesome. That sounds perfect. I needed to get a post card anyway." Claire launched the ball, yet again, and Buck took off with enough energy that you would have thought it was the first time.

"We," Cole nodded to the dog who was trotting back, "are going to be out along the fence line today. So we should be out of your hair, regardless." The man turned away with an air of importance and a hint of annoyance. At least, that was what Claire perceived.

"I didn't mean to offend," she said, slowly turning to fully face him for the first time in the conversation. "I just want to get out and see some of the sites."

Cole, with his back half turned, glanced back at her. She couldn't read his eyes or his body language for that matter.

"Tell Morning Star I sent you." He turned and walked out of her line of sight. A few moments later a sharp whistle cut the air and Buck took off in the cowboy's direction at a dead run.

"Well, I'll be." Claire put her hand on her hip. "I just can't figure that man out." After a moment she walked back into her cabin. "And why I am trying to, only the Lord knows."

* * *

An hour later, Claire found herself driving down the smallest main street she had ever encountered. She had had no trouble finding it. It was the only street in town that had businesses lining both sides. It was cute, though. In a very country kind of way. The hardware store had things out on the sidewalk, as if no one here would ever think of stealing. Next door, a tiny boutique had a rack of clothes. There were flags attached to the few light-posts announcing the county rodeo in August. A bank had a chalkboard sign out front, an old western font announcing free jerky with each new checking account opened.

"We are not in Kansas anymore," Claire half whispered to herself as she parked her car in front of a shop with a sign announcing souvenirs and gifts. "Or maybe we are…" She shook her head as she gathered her laptop case and purse.

The front windows of the shop were stocked with dream-catchers, cowboy hats, all sorts of huckleberry goods, and Montana t-shirts. It was done in a cute, tasteful way. Nothing like some of the gaudy display windows in the city. Claire pushed the door of the shop open and was charmed by the old-time doorbell that announced her arrival.

A beautiful young woman, maybe in her late twenties, early thirties, came out of a back room carrying a stack of books. Her hair was braided into two long braids, and her skin was a lovely dark tan.

"Welcome," the woman said as she positioned herself behind the cash register.

"Are you Morning Star?" Claire asked as she moved to put her things on one of the two small tables set up in a corner.

The woman's eyes narrowed, and she set the books down with a thump. "Who's asking?"

"Oh!" Claire walked over to the register and stretched out her hand. "I'm sorry. I'm Claire. Patrick Cole sent me. I'm staying at his guest cabin."

A warm expression washed over the woman's face and she took Claire's hand into her own. "Sorry," she apologized. "You can get a coffee on me today. You just never can be too careful with strangers, sometimes. Not in these parts."

Claire nodded her head in agreement, but she wasn't entirely sure she knew what the woman meant. She had thought everyone in small towns like this were supposed to be overly friendly and helpful.

"It's my fault," Claire smiled. "I didn't mean to catch you off guard."

"Folks around here call me Kate," Morning Star explained. "Cole has to be the last one around these parts to still call me Morning Star."

"Why?" Claire blurted out before she could remember her manners.

"Oh," Morning Star raised her delicate eyebrows, "makes me whiter to some folks, I suppose."

Now it was Claire's turn to have raised eyebrows.

"Memories go way back and sometimes they are less than accurate." Morning Star shrugged as if it wasn't a big deal.

"Well," Claire said slowly. "Can I call you Morning Star?"

"I'd like that." Morning Star smiled and shifted over to the coffee bar, flipping a few levers and causing steam to bellow from the contraption. "Now, what can I get you?"

Claire took a moment and gazed up at the chalkboard menu. Everything sounded wonderful. "I think I'd like a breve. The biggest you can make."

"Coming right up!" More steam poured out over the coffee bar. As Morning Star went about preparing Claire's coffee, Claire glanced around the shop. It was charming. The same aesthetic that graced the front windows continued throughout the room. There were more trinkets, books on Montana, a small fiction section, beautiful western jewelry.

She was perusing the shelf of books when Morning Star walked around the counter with two giant steaming mugs of coffee. They made their way to the table where Claire had dumped her things.

"How are you liking Paradise Valley?" Morning Star asked as she slid a coffee in front of Claire.

"The mountains are stupendous!"

Morning Star raised an eyebrow as she raised her mug to her lips.

"Sorry," Claire said, feeling slightly foolish. "Writer's habit. I know that no one talks like that, but sometimes things just pop out of my mouth before I can think them through."

Morning Star grinned. "I think that's called being human, dear. I don't know that writers have the sole claim to it." She winked. "The mountains are something very special. If you didn't love them, I would be concerned that you didn't have a heart beating in that chest."

Claire smiled and drank a large gulp of her coffee. "This is wonderful, thank you."

"My pleasure. Besides the mountains, how is the ranch? Cole treating you okay?"

"He seems a little rough around the edges," Claire confided, while trying not to think about the glimpses of his shirtless body swinging an ax.

"He has been through the wringer, that one," Morning Star mused. "We used to be great friends as kids. But ever since his dad split, while we were in high-school, Cole has played things rather close to the vest. Doesn't open up to anyone about anything."

Claire made a noncommittal sound as she drank down more of her coffee. "Surely he confides in his girlfriend." The words were out of her mouth before she had a chance to reign herself in. It was an effort not to slap her hand over her mouth.

Morning Star's eyes twinkled. "A girlfriend? Cole? No. Much

to the disappointment of women all over the county. Hell, women all over the state."

Though questions burned inside Claire, she somehow managed to keep her big mouth shut. She kept her eyes fixed on her coffee and fiddled with the handle. She couldn't believe she had let such a stupid comment slip. She was supposed to be here to work on her book, for heaven's sake. Not to fish around for dirt on her rude cowboy host.

"If you want to listen to the rumor mill," Morning Star continued, "a girl broke his heart years ago, and he has never quite been able to recover. Now instead of risking heartbreak again, he secretly goes to see a rotation of other women from all over the state." She finished the tale with a small chuckle.

"Did you and him..." Claire trailed off before she could ask the whole question, regretting that she had even started it.

"Lord, no," Morning Star stated firmly after setting down her mug of coffee.

Maybe it was her writer's mind, but Claire couldn't help but think that the woman had answered the question a little too quickly, too defensively. She nodded her head and toyed with her saucer. Time for a subject change.

"This place seems pretty quiet," Claire said, glancing around.

"It's a little too early for tourists, yet." Morning Star nodded. "And the old locals don't seem to have much use for my 'fancy' cups of coffee. Sometimes I'll get a few high-schoolers after school lets out. But for the most part, it's pretty quiet in the offseason."

The conversation flowed smoothly between the two women for most of the afternoon. While Claire didn't get much writing done, she did feel like she had made a dependable friend in Morning Star, and the town gossip had given her some ideas for her story. However, something was nagging at the back of her mind about Cole, about the gossip surrounding him.

Claire scolded herself on the drive back to the ranch. She wasn't here for the cowboy – no matter how many butterflies were in her stomach. She must put such foolish notions to bed, once and for all.

7. The Ride

Cole leaned the hay fork against the barn stall and reached down to lift the handles of the wheelbarrow. Mucking out the stalls was not one of the more glamorous jobs on the ranch, but it had to get done just like the rest of it. He had been hiring the Richardson kid from town to come out on the weekends to do the menial chores. But with times what they were, he had had to let the young man go. The disappointment on the kid's face was enough that Cole had immediately told him that he could still come out and ride whenever he liked.

Shaking his head, Cole dumped the wheelbarrow in a pile outside the back barn door. His bleeding heart disappointed him sometimes. He couldn't even let a ranch hand go without offering up a consolation prize. Feeling for the poor kid was all fine and dandy, but wasn't it his bleeding heart that had gotten him into this mess with the ranch in the first place?

Cole's steel-toed work boot came in contact with a bone, which then went skittering across the barn floor. Where was that blasted dog, anyway? It was his job to be chasing the barn mice. Cole did not like cats, and the little heeler did an excellent job of barn-catting. But only when he could be bothered with it, apparently.

Cole puckered his lips and let a sharp whistle cut through the air. He listened, expecting to hear the jingle of the dog's collar racing toward him. But that is not what his ears picked up. What he heard was a female voice murmuring. At first, he was confused, then his mind slowly put it all together. Cole stuck the wheelbarrow inside the barn door and headed toward the guest cabin.

Sure enough, there was Buck, chasing down throw after throw. Claire stood, just as she had the day before, in blue jeans and a t-shirt, with a mug of coffee in hand. Her grin lit up her whole face. Wisps of hair had escaped her braid and framed her face, the sunlight catching them just right. Damn, she was beautiful. For a city woman, Cole scolded himself. He tried to think about her covered in mud. It didn't help.

He couldn't help himself as he walked right up to the edge of the porch. Buck, returning with a bright-green tennis ball, glanced at him, but then continued straight on to their guest. She obliged the mutt and sent the ball flying once again.

"He sure does like to fetch," Claire mused without turning to Cole, her gaze fixed on his dog instead.

"I have no idea where he gets all of that energy from, but he could do this for hours," Cole confirmed. "He would probably want to keep going even if your arm fell off."

Claire chuckled, deep and resonate. It tore Cole's attention away from the dog. He thought women's laughs were supposed to be delicate, gentle, polite little things. This woman's laugh wasn't manly, but it wasn't girly either. It suited her, and Cole, just fine.

"Do you want a cup of coffee?" Claire asked, and Cole realized he had been caught staring. The woman's eyebrows were now raised in an unspoken question.

"Sure, sure." Cole scrambled to not look a fool. "Coffee sounds good."

While Claire disappeared into the guest cabin, Cole tried to pull himself together. Maybe he did need more coffee, just to help him focus, keep his mind off of the fairer sex.

Buck vaulted onto the porch and dropped a tennis ball where Claire had been standing. The dog then flopped himself down next to it. He looked at Cole, grinning, sides heaving, and tongue lolling out to one side of his mouth.

"Traitor," Cole murmured and narrowed his eyes at the dog.

"What was that?" Claire asked as she came out of the cabin, two steaming mugs in her hands.

"Oh, nothing," Cole drawled, feeling the heat sneak up his neck. He was blushing? Good Lord, this wasn't good. This wasn't good at all. "Where did you learn to throw like that?" He attempted to distract them both.

"Oh," Claire said as she bent down for the tennis ball. Buck was on his feet in a heartbeat. "An older brother who played in the minors." She launched the ball and Buck went streaking after it. "He needed someone to practice with when we were kids. I might have been better than some of the boys on his teams over the years."

Claire's eyes twinkled. Cole couldn't decide if she was pulling his leg or not. He guessed not, after watching her throw the ball, yet again, for his traitorous dog.

"I would have hated to play against you," he said, raising the mug of coffee to his lips. "That's for certain."

They both stood in the still morning air, watching Buck trot back with a tennis ball. It wasn't an awkward silence, but Cole could tell there was some sort of tension between them. He didn't know what it was, exactly, but he sure could feel it.

He cleared his throat and downed the rest of his coffee in a couple of gulps, intending to get on with his day. He mentally started making a list of all of the things he had to get done.

"The mountains truly are beautiful." Her honeyed voice nailed him to the spot, and he found that he wanted to keep the conversation going.

"Yeah, they sure are," he nodded out toward the range. "Once they get in your blood, they don't let you go."

"That's a very romantic notion," Claire turned toward him, and he caught the twinkle in her eye, "for a tough cowboy, that is."

"Do you want to see them up close? The mountains I mean." The words were out of his mouth before he even knew he wanted to say them. For Pete's sake Cole, he scolded himself, you've got enough to do without playing tour guide for a tourist.

"What do you mean?" Claire asked with raised eyebrows. "They seem pretty close to me."

"I am riding the fence line this afternoon. Checking for breaks in the line and what not." The words had again flown unbidden from his mouth. But now it was too late to go back. "You are welcome to join me if you are of a mind to."

Claire gave him a half smile and turned to study the mountain range in front of them. Cole didn't know if he hoped she would say yes or say no. What was the matter with him these days? He must be spending too much time alone. Or maybe the stress of keeping the ranch afloat was making him lose his mind.

"I'd like that," Claire said, turning back to him. A beautiful smile lit her whole face and Cole struggled to keep his own face neutral. This was getting ridiculous.

"Meet me over by the corral in, say, two hours?" he asked, nodding back toward the barn.

Claire nodded. "That would be perfect." She raised her coffee mug to him.

"Thank you for the coffee." Cole set his mug down on the porch. "Thank you, ma'am." He turned to walk back to the barn, just before he was out of sight of the guest cabin porch, he whistled for his dog, who came running. At the last second, Cole shouted back toward the cabin, "And don't wear those fancy boots!"

He could hear Claire murmuring something that was probably less than ladylike. Only then did Cole let a sly smile play on his lips.

* * *

Two hours later, on the dot, the door to the guest cabin swung open. Cole and Buck looked up at the same time to see Claire, standing in the same t-shirt and jeans as before and wearing a sensible pair of sneakers. Buck shot toward her. Clearly, Cole was no longer the dog's favorite human. I'll remember that next time I think of buying you a bone, Cole told the dog silently.

"Afternoon," his guest called, tipping an imaginary hat toward him, a smile on her lips.

"Afternoon," he returned the favor and was almost dismayed to feel her smile reflected on his own mouth. He tried to school his face into something more appropriate for a boring tour guide, but Cole doubted very much that he was winning at that game. He patted a horse's flank as he walked around him to greet their guest. The horse whinnied at him, and Cole was pretty sure he was being mocked.

"You just settle yourself down," he muttered to the horse, and maybe to himself too.

"Lovely day for a ride, isn't it?" Claire asked as she came up alongside him.

Cole looked up at the endless blue sky, the bright sun, and said, "It sure is."

He was standing awkwardly in front of the two horses he had saddled, not really knowing what to do next. This is why he never wanted to be a tour guide. Thankfully, his horse shifted and bumped into him, pushing him out of his stupor but also closer to Claire. She grinned at him.

"This here is Scout. I'll be riding him," Cole reached out and scratched the ornery horse's shoulder flank. Scout shook his head in pleasure. Claire giggled, covering her mouth with one hand. It was kind of cute, Cole decided.

"And this is Lady. She is much more loving and gentle," he told Claire as he walked over to the other horse and rubbed the end of her nose. Lady pushed into his hand. Cole smiled at her. He knew having her nose rubbed was one of the horse's favorite things.

Claire stepped up next to him. "I didn't expect them to be so big," she breathed. "In the movies, they don't seem so huge."

Cole studied her before he answered. She was in awe of the horses. He, on the other hand, had grown up around the animals and maybe took them for granted. But he could see through her eyes their impressive size and gentle manner.

"Hold out your hand like this." Cole held his own hand out to the end of Lady's nose. Her velvety skin tickled his hand as she sniffed at it. "It lets her smell you, get used to you being near.

And she likes to make sure you aren't holding out on any apples or carrots."

Claire cautiously stepped forward, holding her hand out in front of her, until she was even with Cole. Their hands touched as Lady's lips brushed against them. Claire gasped, and Cole's eyes jerked to her face, but he saw the light in her eyes and the smile on her lips. The tourist was not afraid as he had expected her to be. She was full of surprises, this woman.

"Hi there, Lady," Claire cooed. "We are going to be good friends, aren't we?" She was now rubbing on the horse's nose in the exact spot where she liked it. Cole let his hand drop away. It was clear he wasn't needed as a mediator between the two.

After a few minutes of petting the horse, Claire looked up at him. The excitement in her eyes took Cole's breath away. He almost forgot how to breath.

"Don't we have a ride to take?" Her teasing voice finally pulled him out of his stupor.

"Yes," he said, while removing his hat and wiping at his forehead out of habit, hoping he wasn't blushing again. "We do have a ride to take."

Cole took Lady's bridal and led her over to a mounting block. Claire walked next to him as if it were the most natural thing in the world. They were both silent, but the silence wasn't heavy. It was peaceful. Lady stopped next to the block, this wasn't her first rodeo, though it was Claire's.

"What is this?" she asked, eyebrows raised.

"It's called a mounting block. You can use it to climb up on Lady, here," Cole explained, holding the horse in place though she didn't really need the guidance. Lady had done this hundreds of times. "It's what we use for the kids who can't mount up yet."

Claire's eyes widened slightly, but then she stuck her tongue out at him before she climbed the mounting block. The woman might be a good sport after all. As she settled on the horse, Cole couldn't help but think about how natural she looked. It was like she belonged on a horse. Much more than she belonged in that tiny rental car of hers, anyway.

"I'm going to hand you the reigns now," Cole explained as he moved. "Lady won't move. She knows what we're about. Don't you girl?" He rubbed the horse's cheek as he handed the leather strap up to his guest. Claire took it without a word, but there was a massive smile on her face. Oh yes, she could definitely belong in this world of his.

Cole shook his head as he walked quickly over to Scout. What had gotten into him? This woman was a city woman from God knows where and a guest on his ranch. It didn't matter how beautiful she was, or how much the mare liked her. There wasn't a damn thing he could or should want to do about it. The pressure of trying to keep the ranch afloat was apparently getting to him.

He mounted Scout in a hurry, already eager to be done with the impromptu tour guiding. Cole brought his horse next to Lady and Claire.

"Let's ride," he said briskly and nudged his stallion forward.

8. The Fence Line

Claire had thought that the mountains were beautiful from the back porch of her cabin, but as they rode closer, the mountains grew into massive god-like beings. And to put it lightly, they took her breath away. The trees ceased to be one big mass of blues and greens as she began to see that each tree was different; each grew differently, had a different face, a different shape. A closer look even revealed a break in those trees, here and there, to reveal rock faces or small cliffs. It was astonishing to see, even there, a tree or two thriving.

Claire had never really seen anything like those mountains. It was more inspiring than she could have imagined. Yes, she would need to write about this. Somehow, someway, she had to find a way to squeeze it into a book. Or maybe a collection of essays like John Muir, though she could never be on his level.

Nature is truly amazing, she thought, but didn't dare say aloud. She didn't want to sound any more like a city slicker than she already did. Stealing a glance at the cowboy, she saw he was as taken with the mountains as she was. Good, she thought, maybe I'm not such a fool after all.

Lady was gentle with Claire as they rode along. She didn't move too fast, always keeping a few paces behind Cole and his mount. The horse's gentle sway was reassuring, comforting; paired with the mountains' majestic presence, Claire thought she could be content forever. But then the man on the horse turned back to catch her eye.

Claire felt the breath catch in her throat at his direct gaze. Then he turned away, saying nothing. She glared at his strong, straight back. His mood swings were becoming quite tiresome. One minute he would be teasing her, playing. The next, he would be silent and brooding. Just like he was now, for instance. Claire could not get a read on him. She forced her mind to push him aside as her lungs sucked in a big breath of mountain air. Not even the man's sour mood could ruin this wonderful experience. Though… he had asked her to come along, so he couldn't hate her all that much. Right?

They rode in silence for what could have been an hour, or it could have been an eternity. Claire was too wrapped up in the beauty of the land to know or care. But as the minutes ticked by, she couldn't help but notice that the cowboy's shoulders had begun to relax. Well, she thought, at least that is something.

"So…" She drew out the word as Lady brought them abreast. "Sure is beautiful out here."

Cole nodded politely, and Claire thought he was going to brush her aside and not say anything. But then he answered in a soft, far-off voice. "Yes, it sure is. There is nowhere else in the world like it."

When he didn't continue, Claire assumed he was going to continue brooding, ignoring her, and leaving her to her own imagination. But something seemed to change in the air, or maybe it was that they were riding abreast now. Either way, Claire wanted to know more about him. Being as curious as she was, and being the writer that she was, she couldn't keep herself from trying to break through the man's crusty exterior. He had an interesting story to tell, she knew it in her bones.

"I can see why you call this Paradise Valley. It is truly a paradise out here," she began, trying to ease into a conversation. "Have you always lived on the ranch?"

"I've lived here all my life. Grew up ranching. Believe it or not, the ranch yard used to be full of activity, but now it's just me." Cole sighed, and Claire thought that that was going to be the end of it. She had pushed the wrong button. His shoulders drooped just the smallest bit, but it made him appear to be much smaller than he really was. How odd, Claire thought.

"My grandfather's father, he bought this little spit of land when there was nothing out here but the wildlife and a handful of hermit mountain men," Cole continued softly, surprising Claire. She had to lean in to make out his words. But then Cole turned to her and smiled. He seemed to speak to her now, more than to his memories. "Some folks in these parts say that they tamed the country. But that's just a load of hogwash. The land taught us how to live here. It will never be tamed." His shoulders straightened as he continued to talk. He sat on his horse taller and seemed prouder as the words poured out of him.

"I can see that." Claire gazed up at the peaks in front of them. She agreed, nothing could ever tame them, of that she was sure.

"We've been raising cattle ever since. Used to have a big herd that stretched as far as your eye could see. Or at least that's what I thought when I was straddling the horse in front of my grandfather." Cole continued while leading the horses to the edge of the fence line, close to where the forest grew out of the prairie land. His eyes studied the fence line, looking for breaks, even as he kept glancing at her, perhaps studying her as well. Claire decided she wanted it to be because he liked her, not because she was a city girl that was sure to ruin everything.

"But things are different now," he trailed off, letting the silence between them grow heavy again.

Finally, Claire couldn't help herself, from her curiosity or from wanting to hear his rich voice again. "Why did it change?" she asked. "What happened?"

"My dad," Cole said with a strong twist of bitterness. "My dad happened. Granddad worked hard, really hard, for years and years, to pay off the land and loans that had been taken out to pay for the growing ranch. He had been squirreling money away for the lean years – which were sure to happen eventually, as he would say.

"The man practically raised me. You see, my dad thought he was some hot shit. He rode broncs on the rodeo circuit, would even win sometimes and then blow all the winnings on God knows what. He sure never contributed to the ranch, that much I do know.

"He had my grandfather's stature and my grandmother's features. Like I said, he thought he was hot shit. The ladies would think he was a real fine catch. And my dad would take them to bed, alright. He'd bed them, but never wed them. They couldn't trap him, as he would say. Wild and free, he claimed. He would always be wild and free.

"When I was about thirteen or so, he came back around. Broke as a joke and looking worse for the wear. He said he'd had a bad string of luck and had seen the error in his ways. Professed that he wanted to make up for everything he had done. So on and so forth.

"Now my grandfather was a forgiving man, but not so much a trusting one. He told my dad he would have to earn his keep. And that's what dad did for a few years. He worked hard and wormed his way back into our lives and hearts. My grandfather even came to trust him enough to think that he was actually going to take over the ranch. I think it was a relief for him. He was starting to get up there in years, and the hard work had begun to take a toll on him."

Claire pictured old, weathered hands gripping the pommel of a saddle or the handle of an ax. Hands that were cracked with age and time. Hands that were strong from years and years of labor, but were beginning to fail. She saw those hands rubbing one another, trying to relieve an ache or pain. Claire let the picture fade from her mind as Cole continued.

"Anyway. We all should have known better. Just as soon as my grandfather put his name on the bank account my dad took out a loan against the ranch and hightailed it out of town. Haven't heard hide nor hair of him since."

Cole grew quiet again, and Claire felt the heaviness of the story sitting between them, like dark weight trying to pull them to the bottom of the ocean.

They had been riding leisurely while the cowboy had relieved this bit of history. It was a sad story to be told against such a beautiful landscape. Claire couldn't sort out what she felt. Awe at the land, or heartbreak for the family, or all the emotions in between.

"How old were you?" she finally dared to ask. She didn't know if it was because she wanted to know, or because she couldn't bear the silence anymore.

"Fifteen. I was fifteen when that son of a bitch took off." Cole almost whispered the words.

Now Claire knew her heart was truly breaking. She could imagine a teenage boy, happy, thriving, believing his dad was back for good. Only to be crushed under the weight of a father who apparently didn't love him at all. It was a terribly sad story. But something in the back of her mind niggled at her. Something Morning Star had said, about Cole going off with rodeo princesses. Surely, he wasn't following in his father's footsteps. The man didn't seem like the type.

"My grandfather got old after that." Cole's voice pushed its way into her thoughts, no longer a whisper but colored with grief. "He had always been so robust, indestructible. But after everything happened, well… he aged quickly. He did what he could to make the ranch right again. But it was an impossible task. He died just after I turned eighteen. Left everything that was left of the ranch to me. It was little more than the land deed and the loan against it." Cole turned his head, just enough that he could look Claire in the eye. She hoped her pity for him wasn't written all over her face.

"It's worth it though," his voice was soft but confident, and a smile tugged at his lips. "This land is everything to me."

The silence between them wasn't heavy anymore. It felt light and electric. Something was there between the host and guest, but Claire couldn't put her finger on what it was.

"It was Julie's idea to rent out the cabin. She figured there are enough rich folk who might want to play dude ranch that it wouldn't be too hard to make some easy money off of them." Cole tipped his hat back and wiped at his brow. His eyes smiled at Claire. "She fixed up the cabin and website, she really did it all. And here you are! Though I wasn't expecting to have guests so far out from tourist season." He sent her another smile. Claire felt it all the way down in her toes.

The writer in her had already built up a novel idea around Cole's story. She couldn't help it – this is what her mind did. But who was this Julie? The man had mentioned her a couple of times now. Perhaps she was one of the women Morning Star had alluded too. Claire's mind churned, turning the possibilities over and over.

An easy silence sat between the two riders. They rode along a stretch of fence that seemed to be right up against the base of the mountain range. Claire couldn't see very far into the forest line. All the trees seemed to come together to shut out the outside world. Maybe to keep outsiders, like herself, out. It was a wilderness, after all.

Just as Claire began to ask Cole a question, a strange, strangled cry surprised them both. And before she could complete a single thought in her head, Claire was flying through the air.

9. The Mountain Lion

The moment Cole heard the mountain lion, he knew there was going to be trouble. For the last few years, he would have a calf or two go missing when the cattle were ranging near this stretch of land. He had known there was a den somewhere up along this part of the fence line. It hadn't mattered too much to him at the time. Cole held to his grandfather's tradition: the land gave them everything they needed; if it needed to take a small thing every once in a while, it was fine by him. Give and take was the law of mountains, as far as his family had been concerned.

Most of the ranchers in the area were appalled by the idea. They shot up any kind of predator that dared to look at their land sideways. As if those predators hadn't been there centuries before a white man set a boot upon the soil, or as if this country could be tamed like a tiny lap dog. No, Cole had never been able to wrap his head around that line of thinking. He would only take action against the wildlife if it became clear they were living solely on his herd or if they were mindlessly killing the cattle. And that had worked for Paradise Valley for decades, near on a century.

But as Cole watched Lady rear herself back, forelegs kicking at the sound waves of the mountain lion's cry, and Claire tumbling off of the mare in slow motion, he wanted to slaughter every "dangerous" creature in the whole county.

Cole vaulted himself off of his horse a millisecond after Claire hit the ground. He winced and shuttered, mid-stride, as his guest's head bounced off the ground and then felt sheer terror as her body lay still.

"Claire!" Her name sounded strangled and choked coming out of this mouth. Every stupid movie scene where someone fell off a horse, hit their head on a rock and was killed, flashed through his mind. He tried to shove the images away as he tripped on a rock and almost fell at Claire's side. His arms windmilled, and he came down heavily on one knee next to his fallen guest.

Claire's eyes were open and blinking. He couldn't see any blood or obvious wounds on her head or body. Thank God, Cole thought. He reached out a hand and gently placed it on her shoulder. The woman's eyes turned toward him and became focused, pupils retracting. It was then that he realized she wasn't breathing.

Her hand shot out and grabbed a fistful of his shirt, right at his collarbone, and used it to try and drag herself up. Cole froze. For the first time in all his memory, he didn't know what to do. Somewhere in the distance, he heard a horse whinny. It seemed to kick him out of his stupor, and he was immediately using the hand on her shoulder to help the poor woman into a sitting position. Their eyes were locked when Claire finally took in a deep, shuttering breath.

Having fully sat up, she leaned slightly forward and continued to take in huge breaths. Cole, somewhat unconsciously, began to rub her back with his hand and murmur to her like he would a frightened colt. His relief at Claire being seemingly unharmed was palpable. It seemed to take several minutes for her to catch her breath, but when she finally did, she leaned into his hand which was still rubbing across her shoulders and back.

"So that's what that feels like," Claire announced, her big brown eyes gazing deeply into his own. He must have raised his eyebrows in question because she continued with an explanation not more than a moment later. "I feel bad for every character I've ever had the wind knocked out of."

Her laugh sounded like magical bells on the wind, and Cole couldn't help but smile. In the ease of the moment, he pulled a strand of hair away from her face and tucked it behind her ear. The gesture surprised him, but Cole didn't see any reproach in Claire's eyes. You'd think I was the one who'd been thrown from the horse and had all of my sense knocked out, he thought to himself. Was it his imagination or did she seem to move in closer to him? His hand moved to the small of her back and stayed there, comfortable.

Claire looked down at her lap and pulled another strand of hair behind her ear. She leaned just a little closer, Cole was sure of it this time. He watched as she looked up at him through her thick lashes. It had the most enchanting effect. He caught a whiff of the soap she used, something flowery, on the breeze. He breathed in deeply, as inconspicuously as he could, praying she wouldn't notice.

Her body felt so solid and warm beneath his hand. How long had it been since he had felt such a fierce attraction to someone? Too long, his heart told him. Not now, his head cut in. There was too much going on, and she was a guest of the ranch for goodness' sake. But even as he thought the words, he was leaning in closer to her. He couldn't pull his eyes away from her beautiful face. The heart shape framed by strands of hair that kept escaping from behind her ears, those beautiful eyes – wide and inviting; her full lips – unpainted and yet the perfect shade of red.

Then he felt something wet and soft against the back of his neck. Understandably, he started. His body jerked up and away from the beautiful woman, who was already half in his arms. His hat pushed forward, and the soft wet feeling traveled up the back of his head. Yet he couldn't take his eyes off of Claire, who was now openly laughing at him. The spell of her face wasn't broken until she scrambled out of his reach and started to stand up, wheezing with laughter.

The fog in Cole's mind cleared more and more quickly the further Claire backed away from him. He realized his horse was trying to get his attention. The soft wet feeling was the stallion's lips – which were not nearly as tantalizing as Claire's. Half annoyed and half amused, Cole stood up and pushed the horse's nose away.

"My head is not an apple." The words were clipped as he looked the horse straight in the eye, but his hand still reached up and scratched behind the horse's twitching ears.

Claire's wheezing had developed into a belly laugh, and tears were beginning to form at the corners of her eyes. Cole didn't think it was quite that funny, but couldn't help but smile and chuckle. Damn horse. He took Scout's reins and then walked over to Lady, who was standing innocently a few feet away. The bright smile on Claire's face when he turned back to her could have competed with the most brilliant sun. She was breathtaking. Even more so with the backdrop of his mountains behind her, and her joy lighting her face.

Cole stood holding the reins of his two horses, looking sheepishly between the fence line, the ground, and Claire. She seemed fine, despite the tumble she had taken. More than fine, really, he told himself as he dragged his eyes away from her face again. Perhaps laughter was the best medicine, he mused, trying to normalize his rapidly beating heart. The silence between them started to feel heavy with the kiss that had been so rudely interrupted. Oh, yes. He had definitely been going to kiss her.

"We'd best walk a spell," Cole pointed out as he started to lead the horses, trying not to get sucked back into staring into Claire's eyes.

Those eyes were currently dancing with amusement. "That whole 'what do you do when a horse bucks you off' adage isn't true?" She threw her hand up over her heart and left her lips in a perfect "O", showing her mock horror. "I thought I was supposed to get right back on."

"That may be true for new riders who are looking to make a habit out of staying on a horse." Cole chuckled at her antics. "But guests who aren't really trying to make a career out of it... well, sometimes we like to take it easy on them."

"Who says I'm not trying to make a career out of it?" Claire said in mock defiance as she fell into step next to him. They started to move slowly along the fence line, the horses trailing behind them while grabbing mouthfuls of the long grass every few yards. A soft breeze pushed against Cole, bringing with it all the smells of a mountain spring.

"Well, I would like to learn," Claire continued when Cole didn't say anything. "Part of the Montana experience, wouldn't you say?"

"Yes, ma'am," Cole conceded after a few moments of thought. The last thing he had time for was teaching a greenhorn city girl to ride. But then she was a lovely distraction from his current woes. An enchanting distraction, he amended the thought. "I suppose we could do that if you like."

"Excellent!" Claire's face was the picture of joy, and she did a happy little hop at his words. Cole couldn't help but grin at her excitement. He was in too deep, too fast, and he was in great danger of drowning.

* * *

Claire cursed herself in her mind. Learn to ride? She didn't have time for such leisurely activities! If one could call being thrown from the back of a horse a leisurely activity. She had a book to finish. A book to start, really, before Grace came out to the mountains and throttled Claire with her bare hands. Now that would be a sight for sure.

It was Claire's stubborn competitive streak that got her into messes like this. Tell her she couldn't do something, and some part of her took over and shouted "I'll show you" to the whole world. It had gotten her into more than one scrape, but it had served her well too. Lord only knew which instance this would play out to be.

The cowboy had settled into a comfortable silence, and Claire found herself stealing glances at his long, muscular frame, and those hands which had held her so securely after she had fallen off the mare. Being close to him had smelled like horse, sweat, pine trees, and maybe a hint of desire. Though that last part is probably just your imagination, she told herself. Would her writer's mind ever let her rest? Probably not, and that was probably a good thing. It was how she made her living, after all.

"We can ride every day if you like, in the late afternoon," Cole suggested and then looked to her for approval. "I have miles of fence line to check, and it should get done as quickly as possible."

"Perfect!" Claire shot him a thousand-watt smile. "It will help me push to get my writing done in the mornings."

A magpie's melody stretched across the prairie land. Claire cocked her head and began to notice the cries of the prairie dogs, the buzz of insects, the breeze humming in her ear. All sounds she would have never heard in the city.

"Why write here?" Cole's question tore her focus away from the prairie's music. "It's not even tourist season yet."

"Ah…" Claire hesitated, wondering how much of her love life she wanted to explain in front of this stranger. He was still a stranger, right? What the hell, she thought to herself, when in Rome.

"I… uh…" she hesitated again, not knowing where to start. "I've been a little distracted for a long while, and I am on a deadline."

Cole made a confirming, comforting sound as if he knew exactly what she meant. Lady, behind them, tossed her head and whinnied like she understood too. Claire took in a deep breath, steeling herself to bare her soul, even though she wasn't entirely sure why she wanted to.

"I was with a guy. It was serious. Probably too serious, too fast. One of those." She sighed. "But I loved him. I thought he was 'the one.'" She waved her hands in the air making air quotes, looking straight ahead, not wanting to know if the cowboy thought that she was just another ridiculous woman.

Even though that was precisely how she was thinking of herself.

"I'll spare you the long, sad, dumb story," Claire continued, trying to keep her voice from wavering and the tears from pricking at her eyes. She was so annoyed with herself that just thinking of Chad still brought up such emotions. "Let's just say his moon was in someone else's sky."

Truth be told, she had caught him with his pants down, no pun intended, and up against his secretary. The plan had been to surprise him for their six-month anniversary. She had picked up his favorite meal from his favorite restaurant and taken it to his office, knowing that he was working late. And there they had been, his hands around her waist, she bent over his desk, moaning like he was the gods' gift to her world. Just the memory was enough to make her sick.

Cole was nodding his head like he understood everything she wasn't saying.

"So I swore off men." Claire choked the words out and didn't miss the flash of something in the man's eyes. "But it didn't matter. I haven't been able to get that jerk out of my mind since. And my work is certainly suffering for it. I should have had this book done months ago. When my editor suggested I get away to try and finish it, I googled a quiet getaway and booked the first thing that struck my fancy. So here I am." She had pushed out the first part of the speech so fast that, when she trailed off, the air felt empty and hollow around her.

"Well," Cole drawled out, finally. "The quiet, I can give you."

There was something about his voice that caught Claire's ear. She looked up and found him studying her, with something like regret in his eyes. Or was that her writer's mind kicking in again?

"The quiet I can give you," he said again and looked away.

Claire couldn't help but feel like the man built a wall around himself with the words. Morning Star's warning about him rang through her mind. Perhaps it was for the best. But she couldn't help but feel a little punch in her gut as they wordlessly mounted their horses and started back toward the ranch.

10. The Invitation

Despite his misgivings about teaching the city girl how to ride, Cole found himself enjoying their afternoon rides. Claire had become quite comfortable in the saddle. Even though she was riding the gentle mare, he had to give her some amount credit. There had not been any more mishaps, tumbles, or tragic accidents. Cole couldn't help but think the little lady might be able to handle herself, after all.

Keeping that thought in mind, he decided he was going to teach her to saddle Lady. She had hinted at it several times, and by hinted he meant she had done just about everything but come out and ask directly. Claire was about as subtle as a gun. But the woman was independent, Cole had to give her that. He didn't think she would ever pawn off something that she could do herself, including getting that little car unstuck from that mud puddle. He still had himself a chuckle every now and again when he thought about that first time he had laid eyes on her, covered in mud and madder than a wet hen.

They were in danger of becoming good friends, he and his

guest. Perhaps something a little more than friends. Cole shook his head and mentally chastised himself. The woman had said she'd sworn off men. And after what she had been through, was it any wonder? To catch your man cheating on you? They had ways to deal with that back in the old days of the West. Being buried up to the neck next to an anthill sounded like a pretty good form of justice to Cole, though he doubted that Claire needed someone to defend her honor.

He kept telling himself that he was only doing for her what he would be doing for any other guest. Stacking the firewood, showing her how to light a fire in the small wood stove in the cabin, that was all fine and well. But taking her on daily rides, giving her the history of his family, letting her smile put a crack in his heart, all of that was pushing the envelope too far. And now he was going to teach her how to saddle a horse? He kept telling himself it was to save time, and he ignored the jump in the pit of his stomach – the one that happened at the thought of being that close to her.

They hadn't so much as brushed hands since she had been thrown from Lady. It was like they both knew they were playing with a dangerous fire that could quickly burn out of control.

"Stuff and nonsense," Cole told the horses as he led them out of the barn and into the bright Montana sun.

"What is nonsense?" Claire asked as she came skipping up to the corral.

Cole looked up sharply, surprised and very glad the woman couldn't read thoughts. Though he had a theory that some women had such power, Claire had yet to show any signs of it.

"Uh…" He scrambled to come up with something that would make sense without revealing all the thoughts spinning around in his head. "Mice already trying to take over the barn?" It sounded like he was answering her question with a question. Smooth. Real smooth, Cole.

Claire raised her eyebrows at him, and he rushed on to explain his ridiculous excuse. "It's spring. Shouldn't be seeing any of those critters until the first snow," he finished lamely. Mentally, he rolled his eyes at himself. No one had ever heard of such foolishness. He couldn't tell if Claire had bought it or not. She seemed focused on rubbing in-between Lady's eyes, the horse pushing into her hand.

"You want to saddle her?" Cole attempted to recover. Claire's brown eyes glanced up to meet his with a piercing gaze.

"Really?" she asked almost shyly.

"Really. I'm tired of doing all the work for you," he teased.

They grinned at each other like a couple of fool teenagers and then she started to hop around in excitement.

"I'll make an excellent John Wayne yet! Or who was female John Wayne? I want to be her."

Tourists are an awfully funny breed, Cole thought to himself, getting too excited for something so simple as saddling a horse. But Claire's excitement was undeniable, and he found that he was just as excited as she was.

"Stay here, I'll be right back," Cole told his guest and disappeared into the barn. He could hear Claire talking to the horse as he grabbed the pad and saddle. He walked back out into the yard and was momentarily blinded by the sun, and the girl who was silhouetted. Oh no, Cole told himself, you've got it bad. He shook his head, as if that was going to ease the crush, and walked over to throw the saddle and pad over the corral fence.

Claire looked up at him, still rubbing the horse's nose, with merriment dancing in those big brown eyes. Cole's heart skipped a beat or two before he reached over and grabbed the pad.

"This goes on first. Protects the horse," he explained, hoping the routine of saddling the horse would distract him. Claire nodded, following his hands with her eyes. "You have to place the pad like this, not too far forward and not too far back. Otherwise, you'll be doing more harm than good."

Claire moved to stand next to him, her hand never leaving the horse. She studied his placement of the pad with the attention of someone who actually wanted to learn. Cole didn't know why, but that surprised him a little. He moved to grab the saddle. The tourist dutifully stepped out of the way so he could swing it onto the mare's back. Again, this surprised him. Maybe she had a knack for ranch life after all.

"You almost look as good as John Wayne doing that." Her voice had a magical, teasing tone to it, but when he turned around, she seemed to realize what she had said. She studied the ground intently, and her cheeks were turning the loveliest shade of pink. He cleared his throat and tried to ignore how beautiful that made her look.

"Next we need to secure the front cinch, like this." He moved on rather than address the comment. He didn't want to cause the tourist more embarrassment. His hands deftly wrapped the leather strap around the securing ring until there wasn't any length left. Then he moved to the back cinch, securing it a little looser than the front. He realized he had stopped explaining things to Claire. Cole turned and found her watching his hands intently.

Before he could stop himself, he blurted out, "I was thinking of having a bonfire tonight."

Claire looked up at him, eyes wide and her lovely mouth pursed into a perfect "O".

He hadn't been planning on having a bonfire. Not in the least. Lord only knew what had gotten into him! But now he scrambled, again, to make his fool ideas believable.

"It would be a good night for it." And it would be. That was true. "You should come." He took a step closer to her – horse, saddle, and lesson wholly forgotten. He was lost in those wonderful eyes, those eyes that made him say all kinds of foolish things.

"Yes, I'd like that," Claire half whispered, her hands nervously held at her side, her fingers fidgeting.

"Good," was all Cole could think to say. "We'd best get going then."

He turned to the mare and reached for the lead that tied her to the fence. Claire cleared her throat and then apologized.

"I'm sorry. I just remembered that I promised my editor that I would call her this afternoon."

Cole turned to see that the nervous fidgeting had gone up a notch or two. Was she worried about him or her editor? Did it or should it even matter?

"Okay," Cole drawled out, still confused – about what was happening, and about why his heart was going about a million beats per minute. Claire turned and started to walk quickly back toward the cabin.

"I'll see you tonight," she called back over her shoulder.

And that was that. Cole huffed to himself and turned to the mare. "I guess it'll be just you and me today, old girl."

* * *

Claire drove her tiny rental car straight to Morning Star's catch-all coffee shop, playing the local classic-rock station at high volume the whole way. She had gotten so flustered with Cole, she had to make an escape before she did something stupid. Claire needed to get her head on straight, cool off, convince herself there was nothing between her and the cowboy. Plus, it wouldn't hurt to have a latte as a treat – a reward for all of the hard work she had been doing. Namely, saddling a horse. She hadn't gotten much further in her novel, but Chad's face seemed to be taking up less and less of her creative space than it had been before. Small miracles.

She pushed the novel from her mind and focused on her invitation to the bonfire. Bad idea. What did one wear to a bonfire? She had never attended such an event. However, she couldn't help but imagine it was a very romantic occasion. It had to be. Well, she really wanted it to be. Blast, there went her writer's mind again, making up things that probably weren't even half true.

Inside the gift/souvenir/coffee shop, the coffee smelled like coffee. No shocker there, but it instantly made Claire feel more at ease. Morning Star held up the milk pitcher in greeting. Apparently, the woman had seen Claire pull up and was already working on their delicious drinks. Claire innocently wandered over to where several pieces of jewelry were displayed. They all had a hint of Native American culture, much like the coffee shop itself, and she was sure they were hand made.

Those silver feather earrings were calling Claire's name, that was for sure. And maybe the necklace with a single turquoise stone. It would be a nice souvenir, she told herself. Of course, she wouldn't buy it just to impress a cowboy at a bonfire. She would never stoop so low. Inwardly, Claire rolled her eyes at herself and then started as Morning Star appeared at her side, two full mugs in hand.

"Jewelry, is it?" Morning Star raised an eyebrow as she handed Claire a freshly made latte.

"I've basically been dreaming of these earrings." Claire took the latte and used it to gesture toward the earrings in question. "But now this necklace has caught my eye too."

"You have good taste," Morning Star moved her head so that she could spy on the price tags and then exclaimed, "Very good taste!"

Both women laughed and then moved toward a table with their coffees. After some basic, friendly chitchat, Claire got right down to business.

"What does one wear to a bonfire?" she asked as innocently and as stealthily as possible.

"A bonfire?" Morning Star looked utterly confused.

"Cole said we are to have a fire tonight. And I don't know what to wear." Claire could feel the blush sweeping into her cheeks as she explained her dilemma. She sent up a silent prayer Morning Star wouldn't be able to tell.

"A bonfire?" Morning Star just repeated her question, but now she was trying to hide her smile behind her mug of coffee. Her long, delicate fingers were holding it tight and her eyes danced with laughter. "You want to know what to wear to a bonfire?"

Claire felt a rush of embarrassment flood her system. She didn't think it was a crazy question, but it sure seemed that Morning Star did. Claire had, once again, proven she was just a city slicker in a world completely foreign to her.

"Where did you come from?" The laughter in Morning Star's voice was kind and gentle, rather than mocking. It put Claire at ease and wiped away her embarrassment.

"Clearly, not from anywhere around here," she said as her

own laughter took over.

"Clearly." Morning Star put down her coffee mug and reached across the small table to take one of Claire's hands in her own like she was comforting a small child. "Around here, we just wear what we have on. Unless it's an engagement party or something. And even then, most folks just put on jeans and a clean shirt."

Claire felt her cheeks blush again. She could see now that it had been a foolish question. Claire blamed how foggy her mind got around that man. Damn it all to hell, what had she been thinking?

"I might buy those earrings and the necklace anyway," she declared. "Not for the bonfire, but because I like them."

"Here, here!" Morning Star raised her mug in a toast. "I won't ever turn away a paying customer."

Claire grinned, and inwardly admitted to herself that she would definitely be wearing them to the bonfire that night. She couldn't help herself.

"How is he?" Morning Star's face had suddenly gone still. She was referring to Cole, of course. Claire couldn't help but wonder if she was one of the women that Morning Star had alluded to before – one of the ones who had been spurned by the cowboy.

"He seems fine to me," Claire said, and then rushed on as she realized how that statement could be taken. "He has been teaching me to ride. I really love it. And I love the mountains. I don't know how I am ever going to leave them."

Morning Star nodded and finished off her coffee. Claire wondered what the woman's story was. She seemed such a lovely person, but maybe also a person with many secrets. However, Morning Star was her only friend within a thousand-mile radius. Besides Buck and Cole, if Cole could even be counted as a friend. Everyone was entitled to a secret or two. But her curiosity nettled at the idea.

The two women chitchatted for another hour – about the weather, the upcoming tourist season, Claire's book, Morning Star's plans for her little establishment. At the end of the visit, Morning Star wrapped Claire's purchased jewelry in little gift boxes. She suddenly looked up and said, "Now, make sure you have your prom dress pressed for that bonfire tonight."

Claire snatched her new purchases off the counter and then stuck her tongue out. "You just never mind what I do at that bonfire."

Morning Star's joyful laughter followed Claire all the way out to her mud-covered rental car.

11. The Bonfire

Cole had seen Claire's rental car pull up to the guest house as he carried another arm full of birch firewood to the fire pit behind the house. Lord only knew what the woman was up to now. He caught himself smiling. Buck, at his feet, looked up at him with mocking eyes.

"Shut up," Cole told the dog and shoved him away with his leg. Whatever he felt, Claire would be gone in a few days. And that would be the end of that. Then maybe he would be able to focus on the ranch again, instead of letting his head float up on cloud nine. He had never been so irresponsible in his life. At this rate, which basically meant tour guiding Claire every day, it would take ten times as long as it should to finish checking the fence line. Though, if she took off to town like she had today, he might be in luck. It was safe to say that he had made up some time today, out by himself. But it had seemed much quieter, almost lonely, without the tourist tagging along.

Buck disappeared as Cole knelt down to start the fire. "Off to see a beautiful woman, no doubt," Cole muttered to himself, stacking the kindling wood in a tic-tac-toe formation. He tried to clear his mind as he put newspaper under the perpendicular pieces of wood and set a lighter to them. As the paper burned, the kindling started to catch and began to crackle. Cole bent down and blew a soft breath onto the small glowing bits of wood to help it along.

The secret with any bonfire was to have it burning good, well before anyone showed up. That way, they wouldn't have to watch you struggle, should the wood be a little too green or wet. His grandfather's theory echoing through Cole's mind brought a smile to his face. Luckily, this wood seemed to be catching just fine. He stood and went to fetch another armful of wood, just in case.

He was moving the grill over the fire when he heard the door on the guest cabin shut. Buck's collar jangled as he ran toward the fire pit. Cole looked toward the sounds and was slightly stunned. He had half expected Claire to have a handkerchief tied around her neck and her jeans tucked into fancy, tourist cowboy boots, some outrageous cowgirl costume. His expectations had been dead wrong.

Instead, she was wearing a simple white t-shirt, half tucked into her plain, tight blue jeans at the front. A lovely, simple necklace graced her neck, and tiny glints of silver reflected off her earrings. The setting sun lit her skin and hair aglow. "Simply breathtaking" were the words that ran through his head over and over, unchecked.

Cole sat back on his heels, a little stunned. Why couldn't she have dressed the part of a tourist? A tourist would be much easier to brush aside and ignore. Hell, she hadn't been much of tourist since that first day with the mud puddle. He was going to have to put a stop to the guest-cabin nonsense immediately if this is what was going to happen. But he knew this wasn't going to happen again. There wasn't anyone like Claire.

Cole was suddenly glad he had changed into a fresh, clean, plaid snap-shirt. He added another log to the fire, under the grill, as she sauntered up. He hoped his hat covered the heat that was rising into his cheeks.

"Howdy," he said by way of greeting, not really looking up to meet her eye.

"Howdy?" She said it like a question, like she wasn't really sure if she should play along with the cowboy game.

The silence felt odd. Maybe neither one of them wanted to admit what had happened at the corral earlier in the day. Or maybe it was something else. Cole didn't dare take a guess. Buck plopped himself down in between the two humans, seemingly content to watch it all play out.

"I hope you are hungry," Cole said, finally looking her in the eye as he started walking toward the house. "It's steak and baked potatoes for dinner. I'll be right back."

"Sure thing," she said, as if it were the most natural thing in the world – two people having a bonfire in the middle of the week.

When he came back out, a tray of food in one hand and a couple of beers in the other, he saw that Claire had made herself comfortable on the log next to the fire pit. He had laid out a southwest patterned blanket on it to make it more comfortable. Plus, with the chilly nights, he thought his guest might need it later.

A memory flashed in his mind. One of him and his grandparents sitting on that very log – roasting hot dogs or marshmallows – just being a family. The whole ranch held memories like that. Now he was the only one left, and he was on the verge of losing it all. It was enough to make his stomach cramp. But he shook his head to clear the thoughts. Tonight, he didn't want to think about any of that. He wanted to eat a campfire steak, breath in the fresh air, and lose himself in the wide-open sky.

"It really is amazing out here," Claire said as he sat the tray of food down on an upturned log.

"Yeah," Cole agreed. "It's enough to make anyone forget their woes." He handed his guest a beer. It was from one of the local breweries. Quite good, if he did say so himself. Dark and smoky, perfect for a bonfire.

"Yeah," Claire said softly, as she accepted the beverage. She took a sip from the open can. "This is really good."

Cole nodded and was secretly happy the woman wasn't one to only drink those nasty wine coolers. How anyone could stomach that rot, he would never know.

They both fell silent, lost in their own thoughts, taking swigs of beer. Cole eventually placed the steaks on the grill and set the tinfoil covered potatoes on the bed of coals. The hissing sounds of the food cooking mixed with the evening songs of birds and insects. It was a wonderful melody – one that Cole didn't know if he could live without.

The weight of the land weighed heavily on his mind and heart, despite his not wanting to think about it. He couldn't lose it all. If he did, he knew he would lose himself. Then what would he be?

"Are you going to turn those steaks?" A soft voice sliced through his troubled thoughts, which fell away as easily as if they were snow under a bright spring sun. Cole's eyes focused. He had been staring at the fire, and he quickly realized that he did, indeed, need to turn the steaks.

"Sorry," he apologized, an automatic response.

"Nothing to be sorry for. You seemed a little lost in thought. And though I like my steak to have a little charcoal taste to it, I figured I didn't want it to actually turn into a lump of the stuff." Cole caught the wink and smile she threw his way. He couldn't decide if she was just trying to make him feel better, or if it was just her nature to tease. Either way, it relaxed him, and he was able to let go of his worldly woes, at least for the evening.

* * *

The steak was the best she'd ever had, much better than anything she'd ever had in cities. And the potatoes! They simply melted in her mouth with their buttery goodness. With the fire crackling and the sun setting behind the mountains, she could not have pictured a more romantic setting. Of course, some part of her mind filed it all away, to be used in some story at a later date.

"That was amazing," she said as she put her plate down to free up her hands to rub Buck's belly. "My compliments to the chef."

"I'm sure he will be pleased to hear it," Cole said in a mild, teasing voice as he reached over and put another log on the fire, which had died down to red-hot coals while they had been eating.

The sun was almost entirely set now, leaving the sky full of streaks of dark blue, purple, and orange. Claire took a deep breath and sighed. She could live like this forever. As long as she didn't have to cook the steaks.

"Is this a standard bonfire?" she asked, with her eyes closed and her head lifted toward the night sky. "I want to know what I can expect for any future invitations I receive." She opened her eyes and looked straight into his, which reflected the dancing firelight.

"I don't know what other people do," Cole admitted. "I tend to stick close to home. There isn't much time for partying. Too much work to be done." After a few moments, he continued, "Though I don't think many folks serve steak cooked over an open fire."

Claire laughed, a sound that seemed to travel over the open air like magic. "I suppose I will only attend your bonfires then."

She watched as a bright smile opened up across his rugged face. There was a dimple on one side of this mouth. How had she missed it before? It made him seem much more charming, the dimple and the smile, than the first time she had seen him. Claire had to admit to herself that she had misjudged him. Maybe she should tell him so.

"I, uh," she started, as Cole stood, looking at the fire, hands tucked into the back pockets of his jeans. "I feel as though I should apologize to you."

He looked at her with raised eyebrows. He apparently had no idea what she was talking about. She sucked in a deep breath, and with arms crossed, she barreled on.

"I misjudged you. I thought you were some stupid, low thinking cowboy when I first met you." Cole's eyebrows rose even further. "But I was wrong. You can make a damn good steak." She tried to turn the last bit into a joke, to try and save herself from the embarrassment of the admission.

Cole looked at her a moment longer, and then threw back his head and laughed. The sound surprised Claire, but she found herself grinning as well.

"You know," he said, trying to catch his breath. "I thought you were one of those dumb tourists that thought we cage the bears and only let them out in the daytime."

"What!" Claire mocked shock, her hand flying to her heart.

"When you pulled up in that tiny car and drove straight into that mud puddle," Cole burst into another round of laughter. He was wiping away the tears from his eyes when he finally caught his breath again, "I just didn't really know what to think of you."

"I'm sure I was a sight." Claire was barely able to hold in her own laughter long enough to choke the words out.

As their laughter died down, Claire realized they were staring into each other's eyes. He from across the fire, and she looking up at him – adoringly she would say, if she were writing this as a scene. The moment seemed to grow heavy, but she couldn't look away. They were in their own orb, the firelight casting a dome of light into the dark night. They could have been the last two people on earth. It was one of those moments.

Then Cole took a step toward her. And then another. Flashes of their almost-kiss flashed through Claire's mind, and she bit down on one side of her lip, nervous but also so excited. The handsome cowboy stood in front of her, holding out his hand. She must have looked confused, because he said, "Come here. I want to show you something."

Claire hesitated, only for a second, and she didn't know why. She placed her hand in his and stood slowly. His hands were rough from years of hard, honest work. She found that she liked them so much better than Chad's soft, fleshy hands that hadn't ever lifted a finger. She had always imagined that rough hands would feel scratchy and hard, like a dog's paws. What ridiculous notions she sometimes had.

After she stood up with Cole's help, he released her hand like a perfect gentleman. But it felt like a loss to her. She fantasized, in the back of her mind, about those working hands stroking the side of her face.

Cole walked out of the firelight and motioned for her to follow. When she stood next to him, he merely looked at her and pointed up. Claire was reluctant to take her eyes from his but was finally able to do so – scolding herself to get a grip. But all thought was wiped from her mind as she looked up at the night sky.

On the Discovery Channel or some of the science shows, they would flash pictures taken by telescopes of places far away in the universe. None of that compared to what Claire saw now. It was like someone had taken thousands of tiny diamonds and thrown them across the night sky. The stars were so bright and so clear, she thought if she put her hand up, she would actually be able to touch them.

Her voice was soft as she said, "I've never seen anything like it."

"Yeah," Cole breathed reverently. "No city lights here to dim them."

They stood staring into the bright stars for what could have been hours, as far as Claire was concerned. She was consumed by the sight, by her arm brushing lightly against Cole's. You have to stop this silly, schoolgirl obsession, she told herself sternly, even as she wished for more. The goosebumps were surely from the chilly spring air, not her unfounded attraction to the man.

"You are cold." Cole's voice softly pushed its way into her thoughts.

Claire pulled her arms up and crossed them across her body, rubbing them lightly to vanquish the chill. "It's not that bad. And it's worth it," she said as she kept her head turned up toward the sky.

Cole walked away but was soon back with the blanket that

had been on the log. He stood in front of her and draped it around her shoulders. His hands held the blanket, even as she stopped rubbing her arms so that she could clasp it in front of her.

"Do you like to dance?" His question was the last thing Claire expected to hear.

"Excuse me?" she stammered because she didn't know what else to say. She wasn't even really sure she'd heard the cowboy correctly.

"I asked if you like to dance." He was rubbing his hands up and down her arms now, the blanket the only thing separating intimate skin-on-skin contact. Presumably, he was trying to help her get warm again. He needn't have worried. Her whole body was aflame under his direct gaze.

"I… ah…" Claire scrambled to get her mind to focus. "I'm not very good. In fact, I've been told I'm terrible."

Cole's eyes narrowed, and his hands gripped her elbows. "Did that jackass, Chad, tell you that?"

She was surprised at the venom in his voice. "Actually, yes. He did. At a Christmas party."

"I think it's safe to throw anything he said in the garbage. And then maybe light it on fire." His arms were moving up and down hers again, but slower now. "It's really easy," he told her. "Mostly you just sway back and forth."

"No line dancing in Montana?" Claire asked, raising one eyebrow and praying he couldn't tell what effect he was having on her.

"Not tonight. Not here." His voice was solid and certain. Claire wished she felt the same. His arms slowly encircled her, and he began to hum. It wasn't a tune Claire knew, but somehow it felt familiar to her. The way the whole ranch, and the mountains, and the stars were starting to feel familiar to her.

She forced herself to look up into the sky again, but she could feel Cole's eyes locked on her face. His style of dancing really was just swaying back and forth, turning in a slow, imperfect circle. Claire almost felt intoxicated with it all.

How she ended up with her arms around Cole's middle, and her head resting on his chest as they danced, she didn't know. What she did know was that they stayed that way until the fire had almost died out and was only putting off the smallest red glow from the ashy coals. Buck laid next to that fire, watching them, seemingly enchanted as well.

Claire didn't want it to end. She wanted to stay in Cole's arms forever. But eventually, the cowboy stopped humming. He held her for a few moments longer and then pulled back a little bit, looking down into her face. Claire was sure he could read the unbridled desire there, under the light of the stars.

"We are almost finished with the fence line," he said quietly. "I'll see you tomorrow at the corral."

He made sure the blanket was securely wrapped around Claire. The way he looked at her, she was sure he was going to kiss her. But he turned around and walked to the ranch house before she could form any words to call him back. Buck looked at her with forlorn eyes, reflecting the starlight, and then trotted after Cole.

Claire walked slowly back to the cabin. "Some wordsmith you are," she said aloud. "You just stood there like a frog on a log and let him walk away! Without one word."

She moaned in frustration and longing of that kiss she was sure had been coming. "Stupid, romantic night sky," she said as she looked up at the stars again before walking into the cabin.

Yet, despite her frustration, she resolved to write a romantic bonfire scene is some future novel.

12. The Turn of Events

The next morning, Claire virtually woke with the sun. Well, not precisely with the sun, maybe an hour or so after it had crested the mountains surrounding the valley. But it was still earlier than she would have ever even considered opening her eyes were she back in the city. In fact, she still didn't want to open her eyes. She would have much rather continued reliving the fairytale dream of dancing under the starlight.

It really had felt like a fairytale. Cole's big hands softly holding her underneath the blanket he gave her to keep warm. After a few moments, she hadn't really needed the blanket any longer. Claire had been plenty warm, with a blush that she was sure Cole had been able to see, even with the night as dark as it had been – just dark enough to let the stars shine brilliantly. The deep melody he had hummed vibrated through his chest and into her soul as she had leaned against him. How was anyone supposed to wake up and face the real world after something like that?

Coffee. That was the answer. Lots of coffee.

Claire slowly opened her eyes, letting them adjust to the light before she struggled over to the coffee maker. As the coffee pot gurgled, she decided against a shower. Her hair smelled like a campfire. She dreamily brushed it with her fingers, holding it to her nose, breathing in deeply. They say smell triggers more memories than anything else.

Lord only knows how long she stood there. Long enough for the coffee to finish, that much was certain. Claire sighed and forced herself to move. The coffee seemed darker and richer than it had before. Hell, the whole world seemed more alive. Maybe that's how it looked when one got up this early. Then again, maybe not.

Buck was patiently sitting in front of her door when she wandered onto the back porch. A bright green tennis ball lay at his feet.

"You are relentless." Claire sighed as she picked the ball up and threw it as hard as she could muster this early in the morning. Buck took off at his usual lightning speed. She couldn't help but laugh at his enthusiasm as she raised her coffee mug to her lips.

The sun felt good on her face, and she closed her eyes, soaking it in until a wet ball dropped onto her bare foot.

"So demanding!" She picked up the ball and launched it again. Buck disappeared into the grass. It wasn't too tall yet, but he was a little heeler, and he moved too quickly for Claire to follow.

"How does that dog get you to smile like that?" Cole's voice almost startled Claire, save that she had been half dreaming of it since he had walked away from the bonfire.

"Are you kidding?" Claire asked over the top of her almost empty coffee mug. "With that little grinning face of his? How could anyone resist?"

They smiled at each other. Claire thought they both seemed at a loss for what to say next. Maybe neither of them wanted to address what they were feeling. The silence dragged on as Buck came into view, charging back to them with the green ball gripped tightly in his canine teeth.

"Would you like—" Claire began to offer, but Cole held up his own coffee mug before she could finish. "Oh. I guess I'm not entirely awake yet." She offered up a small smile and glanced up at him through her eyelashes. He was just as attractive as he had been the night before. Damn it.

"Figured I didn't want to make you waste all of yours on a poor cowboy like me," he smiled, a dimple creasing as the corner of his perfect mouth.

"Hogwash!" Claire tried not to stare at the adorable dimple and mostly failed. "Is that what the locals out here would say?"

Cole laughed – a deep, rich sound that seemed to fill the valley. Or at very least it filled the crater Chad had left in her heart. What a foolish notion, Claire scolded herself, but only half-heartedly.

They smiled at each other. Cole opened his mouth to say something, but the ringtone of Claire's phone cut him off. They both stood still as if waiting to see what would happen.

"I should get that," Claire admitted reluctantly.

"Of course. I have chores to do anyhow." He turned and walked away, giving Claire a perfect view of his behind – which fit perfectly into his jeans. Before she could lick her lips, the ringtone cut through her thoughts with a loud urgency.

Claire practically ran to catch it before the phone sent the caller to her voicemail. She didn't even have time to glance at the caller ID before she thumbed over to answer the call. Her mind was spinning ideas about summer romances and how maybe this one could work out for her.

"Yes? Hello!"

"Claire. We need to talk." Grace's voice did not sound the least bit like she had enjoyed a romantic evening the night before. In fact, it sounded like it was announcing the long-dreaded zombie apocalypse.

* * *

He'd had both horses saddled for several minutes before she made her appearance. After tussling with Buck, he was about to give up hope, when he caught a glimpse of her out of the corner of his eyes. Or was it the slamming cabin door he heard first? Either way, he was glad to see her.

Cole had trouble sleeping the night before. His mind had been full of fanciful thoughts about dancing and holding a beautiful woman in his arms. He'd been up with the sun, as he always was, but he seemed to have an extra kick in his step today.

Claire stomped up to Lady with barely a glance in his direction and swung up into the saddle. "Are we going to ride or stand here all day wasting time?"

Cole looked up at her sharply, his muscles tensing up. That tone set his teeth on edge. He studied her for just a moment, before mounting his own horse. There was a hard edge to her face that hadn't been there that morning, and her mouth was set in a grim line. She was wearing sunglasses, which she had never done before. It made her feel distant, cold. The day suddenly felt a lot bleaker than it had a few minutes ago.

They rode out of the ranch yard without a backward glance or a word to each other. The prairie land stretched out before them, as far as the eye could see, until it met with the edge of the forest. The mountains seemed to be looming there, just out of reach.

"Are you feeling okay?" Cole finally gathered the courage to ask. They had been riding in silence for more than ten minutes.

"Why wouldn't I be?" she snapped back at him. He had an image of an alligator snapping its jaws down on some unsuspecting prey. Cole scrambled to think of a good answer, the right answer.

"I don't know," he finally said, looking straight ahead at the fence line they had finally come to. Claire didn't deign to acknowledge his words.

How they had gone from smiling and teasing that morning, and dancing and holding each other the night before, to this cold, angry silence, Cole could not even begin to guess. All the delicious tension that had been brewing between them suddenly felt like a boulder in the pit of his stomach. He mentally scolded himself. It's not like they were dating, or even trying to. He had shown his guest a good time while she was in his care. That was all.

Well, he would keep trying to show her a good time. Because that was what hosts were supposed to do. He would be damned if her bad day would ruin his. He nudged his horse to move a little faster. The sooner he got back to ranching and stopped hosting, the better.

"I think we can move a little faster through this section," he explained to his guest. "It was repaired last spring and should have held up without any issues."

Claire only looked at him with a blank expression on her lips. He hated the sunglasses. Without those expressive eyes looking into his, he felt like she was a stone statue. But she urged her horse to keep pace with his.

"I have a lot of work to get done," she finally graced him with the sound of her voice. "The quicker we get this over with, the better."

The quicker we get it over with? Cole thought. He could feel the irritation rising in his chest. He didn't have time for this nonsense. He had a ranch to run and save from being foreclosed on. He certainly didn't need to babysit some city girl who only cared about her own entertainment.

"I didn't twist your arm, you know," he tried to keep his voice even. "Riding was your idea."

Claire's head snapped toward him. Cole could feel the heat of her glare even through the sunglasses.

"Guest-ranch host, my ass," she seethed.

Cole opened his mouth with a hot retort, but she cut him off. "I don't need this bullshit today," she declared. "I'll leave Lady in the corral for you to deal with, cowboy."

And with that, she was gone. She nudged her horse into a trot and was out of earshot within seconds.

Cole's hands gripped the pommel of his saddle so tight his knuckles turned white. His mouth set in a hard, thin line. His eyes narrowed as he watched Claire ride away, her hair streaming out behind her.

"Women." The word seemed dead on the air.

Cole turned his horse toward the fence line. At least he would be able to pick up the pace. Without playing tour guide, he should be able to finish checking the whole fence line that day.

"Huxs," he hissed, pushing the horse into a trot.

13. The Bar

Cole raised the cold mug to his lips and took a deep swig of a local microbrew. The neon signs above the bar announcing Budweiser and Coors cast a depressing glow, giving him a bit of a halo in his reflection in the bar mirror. Big-name brands be damned, he thought. He licked the foam line from his upper lip. It was only his first beer, but he was starting to get that fuzzy feeling in the pit of his stomach. Or had that been there all day?

After finishing the fence line, he had come back home to find Lady in the corral, her saddle and bridle hanging on the fence post. He had snorted at them and glanced at the guest cabin. He could feel her eyes watching him. In fact, the window curtain moved, and he had caught a glimpse of her hand. But nothing more – no apologies or explanations.

Cole had decided he needed a break, an afternoon where he wasn't playing host and where he wasn't thinking about his ranch being foreclosed on. Now he was sitting on a worn-out barstool, alone, drowning his sorrows in a rich Cold Smoke beer. Most of the other patrons had steered clear of him when he entered, as if his black mood was written right there on his forehead.

No matter, he thought as he took another swig, I've always done better alone anyway. He didn't want to discuss the particulars of his life anyhow. Not with anyone. As far as he was concerned, it was no one else's business. Why he had told Claire as much as he did, he would never know. Damn it. He didn't want to be thinking about her right now either.

As the thought was passing quietly through his mind, who else should walk in the door but Mr. Foster. Cole had to hold back a groan and an exaggerated eye roll. Of course Mr. Foster would need a drink after his long, hard day. The man gave Cole the briefest and smallest of nods as he walked by, headed to a back corner table of local business owners. Cole thought he could see a tiny smile plucking at the man's tiny lips.

"It's not over yet," he muttered as he picked up his half-empty pint. The old man couldn't crow yet. He didn't understand what Cole was made of.

Cole gulped down the rest of his beer and started to go for his wallet. He wasn't going to stay and let the man survey his handiwork. But just as he reached for a twenty in his billfold, he sensed someone sitting down next to him. Anger shot through his body and he turned, ready for the fight.

Instead of Mr. Foster, or one of his cronies, it was Morning Star who sat down next to him. She caught the bartender's eye and held up two fingers. Once she was satisfied their beers had been ordered, she half-turned to Cole, cracking open a peanut shell and tossing the nut into her mouth.

"Hiya, Cole," she said, mischief bright in her eyes. "Been awhile since I've had a beer with you. Come to think of it, it's been a while since I have even seen you!"

"If you knew what was good for you, you'd probably steer clear of me today," he replied, picking up the beer the bartender sat down before him.

"Oh, come on now," she said, holding up her own beer. "Cheers! To those of us who work hard every goddamn day."

Cole couldn't help but grin and raised his glass to the toast. He knew Mr. Foster would have heard her sharp words. And he knew that she had said them for the old man's benefit. Good. Let him stew for once. Let him take a dose of his own medicine.

The beer felt good sliding down his throat, cold, frothy, and heavy. It eased some of the tension in his shoulders. He started to relax, finally.

"So, why are you here?" Morning Star asked, her face the picture of innocence. And just like that, Cole had his guard up again. Morning Star always could tell when something was bugging him. "It's not like you to day-drink. Not that I ever remember, anyhow."

"I could ask you the same thing. Don't you have a shop to run?" he said defensively, raising his glass and watching the foam as he swirled the dark liquid.

"This town is deader than a doornail. Besides," Morning Star raised her glass toward the front window, "I saw your truck and mutt outside. I thought I would say a friendly hello. Catch up."

"Well, hello. But I have to be going." Cole reached for his wallet again. He had too much work to do to be wasting time day-drinking. That part Morning Star had right.

"What's got you in such a dark mood?" Morning Star drank heartily from her glass. Cole had always liked that she didn't prescribe to "ladylike" ways. People around town had always whispered that she danced to the beat of her own drum, pun intended. Closed-minded idiots, all of them. As for himself,

Cole had always thought she had a lot of balls staying here and opening that shop of hers. She was a brave woman, no doubt about that.

"Nothing," he answered her question with a bitterness that he could almost taste.

"You used to get that same look back in school. Mostly when things weren't going your way. With a girl, perhaps." Her eyebrows raised with an unspoken question, suspicion.

"Women." Cole couldn't help but roll his eyes. "I am going to swear them off completely. Nobody has time for that kind of nonsense."

Morning Star laughed, a deep and rich sound, but today it grated on Cole's nerves.

"That's not what the rumor mill is saying," she told him, whispering as if it were a conspiracy theory.

"What rumor mill?" he asked, then gulped down half of his beer.

"You know what I am talking about." Morning Star gave him a knowing look with a raised eyebrow. "Word on the street is that you've bedded half of the rodeo princesses this side of the Mississippi."

"Bullshit," Cole said with more venom than he intended. "I ain't my father." He gripped his glass so hard that for a moment he thought it might shatter. He would never be like his father. Never. He'd sooner cut off his right arm. Maybe his left arm, too.

"I'm sorry," Morning Star said after looking at him for a long, hard minute. "I shouldn't push your buttons. But that is what they say."

The silence between them grew. The sounds of the bar and country music filled in the gap, but the air felt heavy, toxic.

Morning Star moved to push on his shoulder. "Come on now! It's just this town. It's how they talk."

"Yeah, this town." Cole sent a meaningful glare in the direction of Mr. Foster's table.

"So what's new with you, anyway? Heard you had a guest staying out there."

"Yeah," Cole gripped his glass hard again. "A guest."

Morning Star raised her eyebrows and turned to face him. "A beautiful guest, from where I am sitting."

Cole raised his eyebrows in question and looked at her from the corner of his eyes. Lord only knew what the woman was thinking. After his recent experiences with that fairer sex, he didn't even want to venture a guess.

"She has been in my shop a few times now," Morning Star confessed. "I like her."

"That's because she doesn't play Jekyll and Hyde with you." The words popped out of his mouth before he even had a chance to think them through. But now that he had said them, he realized they were true. That's exactly how her bait and switch earlier had felt.

"Jekyll and Hyde," Morning Star chuckled, "Come on, Cole."

He shot her a dark, dark glare and it froze the smile on her face. Confusion tangled in her eyes.

"What are you talking about, Cole? Claire is a sweet thing. I bet she doesn't have a mean bone in her body."

Cole gulped down the rest of his beer in one long gulp and practically slammed his glass down on the bar. He turned to Morning Star, and the words came pouring out of him.

"One minute everything is fine. Dancing, starlight, bonfires..." he trailed off.

"Ah yes, I heard something about a bonfire."

Cole raised his eyebrows at his childhood friend, and when she didn't continue, he pushed ahead, not even thinking about the words he had bottled up.

"That stupid tourist is a huge pain in my ass. All of a sudden she wants riding lessons, and to be my friend. Hell, Buck even likes her more than me now. And I am the one that feeds him!"

Morning Star looked like she was trying very hard to suppress a smile, but Cole didn't care. He was too worked up now, the buzz from the beer fueling his emotions and loose tongue.

"I suppose none of that really matters. Because we had a deal. We signed a contract. Claire is a guest. I am a host. And that is how it is supposed to be. No 'ifs.' No 'ands.' No 'buts.'" He trailed off again as the bartender put another cold beer in front of him. Cole took a moment to gather his thoughts. Morning Star waited, apparently in no hurry.

"I'm sorry," he finally said softly, after a swig of beer. "I guess that tourist makes me kind of crazy."

"Yeah, yeah," Morning Star said, taking her own swig. "I suppose she does. But since you are still sitting here, I'm going to tell you what I think." She looked him straight in the eye and made sure he was listening before she continued.

"I think that tourist has surprised you. I think you like her. And I think that terrifies you."

"Like her? Like her!" Cole almost spit out his beer with the words. What an absurd idea.

"Yes, you like her." Morning Star confirmed, looking quite sure of herself. "And I don't think you know what to do about that."

Cole didn't confirm or deny her statements, he just brooded. More than a few minutes passed. Morning Star continued to sip her beer, as he studied their reflections in the mirror behind the bar. There was merriment in her eyes that could not be denied. The woman was turning into a regular Cupid, Cole thought, but kept the thought to himself. Finally, she broke the silence between them.

"If you want my advice, and I don't think you do, but I am going to tell you anyway. You ought to run with it. Have a little fun."

"Fun..." Cole mused. This afternoon had not been fun.

"Yeah, cut loose. Stop focusing on the ranch so much. Enjoy a little bit of your life, before you are too old." She pushed his arm with the last words, before finishing her beer. "I'll let you buy this one."

When he raised his eyebrows at her, she said, "As payment for my sage advice."

He nodded and focused on the beer in his hand.

"But seriously, Cole. Give yourself a break." She put a hand on his shoulder in encouragement, and was gone.

Cole finished up his beer, settled the tab, and walked out to his truck. His mind spun on the drive home. He didn't think he really deserved a break, or a beautiful woman like Claire, Jekyll and Hyde or no. But he couldn't get her out of his mind. Even with her dramatics today, it only made him crazier because he didn't know what was wrong – didn't know how to fix it for her.

He sighed heavily as he turned off the highway, heading toward the ranch. Maybe Morning Star was right. Perhaps he did need to cut loose. Maybe he needed to tell Claire how the whole world seemed to dim around her. No, that would be ridiculous. But perhaps he could tell her that he thought there might be something between them. Yes, that sounded like a much better plan.

Cole parked the truck in front of the main house and didn't look toward the guest cabin as he got out. Now was not the time to try and have that conversation. But soon, very soon. He walked into the house feeling much lighter than he had in days. It must be the spring weather, because there was no way in hell it was the tourist, he thought. Denial could become his specialty.

14. The Grocery Store

The air conditioning felt good blowing down on his skin as he crossed the threshold into the grocery store. He hadn't checked what the temperature was supposed to be, but if he had to bet, he would say it was approaching eighty-five Fahrenheit – a hot day for Montana spring. A sheen of sweat covered his arms below the rolled-up sleeves of his button-up shirt. He pushed his hat back with one hand and wiped at the beaded sweat there as he grabbed a small basket for his purchases.

Even though the temperature had dropped below freezing overnight twice this week, it was a going to be a hot spring day. Welcome to Montana, where the weather will change fourteen times within an hour. One time, Cole had even seen lightning in the middle of a snow storm. The unpredictability of it all was one of the best things about this part of the country, and one of the scariest as far as all the tourists were concerned. Heaven forbid they book a trip and get rained on the entire time. As if anyone here could tame the wild country. Please.

He also loved that he lived so far out of town. Being away

from the hustle and bustle of the little tourist town was much better than trying to live in it every day. Even more so when those tourists took over, year after year – from Memorial Day to Labor Day, like clockwork. But today he was in town for the second day in a row. Which never happened. He should have stopped to get groceries when he had been in town to visit the bar the day before. Unfortunately, it was just another example of how Claire had made him lose his mind.

Cole sighed as he wandered over to the pasta aisle. He hadn't seen his guest since their incident the day before. She wasn't out throwing the ball for Buck this morning. Nor had she come out to take their customary afternoon ride. He knew she was alive though. He could smell the coffee brewing when he walked past the guest cabin.

He was almost okay with not seeing her. He wasn't quite sure what he was going to say to her yet. He didn't know how to express his feelings to her. It wasn't like he loved her, but he was very, very attracted to her. That, at least, he could admit to himself.

Cole picked up a couple of boxes of spaghetti noodles and tossed them into his basket. The sauce was next. Aisle six, maybe? He stood there, glancing over all the different flavors. Why did there have to be so many? His stomach rumbled. Maybe he should have eaten something back at the ranch before this little excursion. Wasn't there an old adage about that? Never shop when you are hungry? Donuts sounded pretty good. Maybe he would just get some of those. His stomach grumbled in agreement.

"The garlic and mushroom is the best one." The voice was sweet and low as it tore his attention from the rows upon rows of spaghetti sauce. He turned to see Claire, holding a basket of her own, standing at the end of the aisle, with a sweet, innocent smile on her face.

"Oh?" Cole couldn't help but add a teasing tone to his question. "Fancy meeting you here. In the spaghetti aisle."

Claire raised her basket and her eyebrows. "I was getting low on food and, more importantly, coffee. Mustn't run out of the magic formula that helps me get the work done."

He smiled, imagining that she was like an angry bear if she didn't have her coffee. Picking up a jar of spaghetti sauce, at random, he started to walk toward her. To his horror, her basket was full of cans of mini ravioli. And not even the good stuff; it was off-brand.

"Tell me that's not what you are buying."

Claire laughed, and Cole's stomach did flips. How could he have missed that sound so much? It had only been a day or so. Perhaps he really was cursed. The scary dragon tourist had cursed him.

"Yes. I like them!" Claire defended herself. An evil gleam showed in her eye as she said, "And I like to eat them cold out of the can."

"I was going to invite you to dinner. But it would clearly be a waste if you love cold, fake pasta out of a can. I think I will buy a box or two of donuts instead."

Her face turned from teasing to utter surprise. Her mouth forming the perfect little "O". Truth be told, he was just as surprised at his words as she was. He didn't think he had been planning to invite her to dinner. Had he?

"Dinner…" Claire said after giving her head a little shake. He noticed she gripped the handle of the shopping basket harder. Why were her hands so cute? "Dinner would be lovely."

Her eyes seemed wide and innocent. Cole could lose himself

in them for centuries. They had probably stood there a few moments too long before he finally snapped himself out of it. It would be rude to take the half invite back, now.

"I'm not the best cook," he said at last. "But I would be happy to save you from yourself." He eyed the nasty contents of her basket again. Disgusting.

"I don't suppose I'm the kind of girl who ever turns down free food. I'm sure not going to start now." She shrugged and chuckled at her own wit.

"Good." He couldn't help the giant smile that spread across his face. It must have been contagious because Claire smiled up at him too. "Shall we say six?"

"Sounds good to me. What can I bring?"

"Not any of that." He raised his basket toward hers and faked a gagging motion.

"Oh, come on," she teased. "It's not all that bad."

He raised his eyebrows at her before pretending to vomit all over the linoleum floor.

"Okay, okay!" She pushed his shoulder. "I get it. You don't need to act like an eight-year-old."

"You would know what an eight-year-old looks like. You clearly never grew out of what they like to eat."

This time she slugged his arm. He just grinned, ignoring the fact that she was stronger than he would have guessed.

"Fine." Her eyes flashed with merriment and mischief. "I'll be at the main house, six o'clock sharp."

"You do that."

"Fine," she said, turning toward the bakery section.

"Fine," he said, not missing the smiles on either of their faces. He watched Claire until she was out of sight. Then he looked down at his basket. Cole figured he should step up his game.

Anything was better than that crap she was buying, but jarred sauce dumped onto noodles was hardly something you should cook for a date.

A date? Was this a date? He supposed only time would tell. Stupid Cupid should have known better than to mess with a lonely cowboy's life.

* * *

The bottle of whiskey felt heavy in her hand as she climbed the three steps onto the main house's porch. Buck appeared out of nowhere and trotted up to her, demanding a greeting. She bent down to pet him, murmuring sweet nothings. Claire was nervous, though she couldn't entirely identify why.

A whistle cut through the air and Buck took off at a dead run around the wrap-around porch. Claire decided to follow him, knowing that he was headed to wherever her host cowboy was. It would, at least, save her the ritual of ringing the doorbell and plying all of the normal niceties. She would much rather avoid the awkwardness that would inevitably create. Not once had they done anything according to usual social standards while she had been here anyway. And she found that she liked it that way.

The main house felt even bigger as Claire walked around its perimeter on the porch. If she had to guess, she would say it had been hand built decades ago. But it had clearly been well cared for. The logs had been stained recently and felt smooth to her touch. To grow up in such a home… she couldn't imagine.

After rounding the final corner to the back of the house, she saw a screen door. As she neared it, she thought she could hear Cole's deep voice humming. It sent a thrill through her body as it remembered what it felt like to be leaning against his chest, feeling that hum vibrate through him. Her chest tightened. Summer fling, here I come, she thought.

Claire knocked on the door frame and opened the screen door. As Cole turned from the counter and smiled at her, her nose was assaulted with all sorts of wonderful spice aromas. Her mouth immediately began to water, though, for the food or the cowboy, she couldn't tell. She didn't care either.

"Hi," the dimpled cowboy said, raising a knife in greeting. He was wearing his typical jean button-down combo, but also had on an apron with the print of a very unrealistic girl's body. She must have been gaping at it, because he looked down and then said, "It was Julie's idea of a Christmas gift."

Claire stood just inside the door frame, not knowing what to do. Her nerves had kicked in, and she craved a shot of the whiskey she held. She felt Cole's gaze travel up and down her. She suddenly wished she had worn more than jeans and a t-shirt. But she had been busy trying to write, trying and failing. She hadn't had time to plan a better outfit.

"Come on in." Cole broke the spell that had her frozen in the doorway. A blush spread across her cheeks as she realized she had been staring at him. She took a few steps forward and set the bottle of whiskey on the kitchen island.

"Whiskey, eh?" The cowboy looked down at the bottle. "My kind of girl." He looked up at her, a twinkle in his eye, and for a moment, Claire thought the world had stopped turning, right then and there.

"I couldn't very well bring a can of fake pasta," she sassed him. Cole burst into a big bout of laughter. Claire couldn't help but join in. And just like that, they were both relaxed and having a good time. Everything felt normal again, just like when they rode together, or their morning coffee/fetch sessions, or at the bonfire.

"What's for dinner?" Claire asked, relieved that she had found her tongue again.

"Ah…" Cole raised his eyebrows. "It's already on the table. Just through there." He pointed with his knife at a doorway off to their left. "Go ahead," he urged. "I'll be right there. I'm just going to finish up this salad."

Claire nodded and started to head in that direction. The house was just as well taken care of on the inside as it had been on the outside. The kitchen was enormous with all of the modern appliances. The doorway led straight into a dining room. She paused to take it all in.

An antler chandelier hung over a rather large dining table. Without counting, she knew the table must sit twelve or fifteen. There was a buffet table in one corner holding a tray of assorted liquors, just like an old western movie. A few framed artworks adorned the walls, mostly pictures of mountains and rivers. It was enchanting. That was the only word for it, Claire decided.

Buck came from the kitchen and went trotting past her, presumably to find his favorite bone and dog bed. He had a rough life. But his entrance and exit pulled her attention back to the kitchen, where Cole was humming. Again. Her legs felt like they might turn to Jell-o.

She stumbled toward the end of the large dining table, where places had been set. It was a formal setting, which surprised her. Two forks, two plates, two glasses, spoon, knife, napkin. The only thing that was missing were the candlesticks.

Low and behold, Cole strode into the room with a candlestick holder that looked very much like Lumiere from Beauty and the Beast. He set it off to the side of the two place settings and lit the candles with a book of matches he pulled from his back pocket. The tiny flames reflected in his eyes as he met her own.

He waved a hand to the table and said, "Lady's choice" before heading back to the kitchen.

Claire was a little too stunned to say anything in response. Who was this guy? A formally set table? Candles? She could hear all of the characters she had ever written cheering her on in her head. They knew how romantic this was. So why couldn't she wrap her head around it?

She moved to the side seat – Cole had set the end place and the one next to it – and sat down. Her eyes traveled over the room again. This was a fairytale. It had to be. A cowboy western fairy tale.

Cole came back into the room carrying a salad bowl and a pitcher of cucumber water. He smiled at her as he set them down and took a seat himself. He indicated that she should dish herself first. Claire complied, still trying to find her tongue.

The cowboy raised his fork to her in salute and declared, "Bon appetit!"

Claire grinned and dug into one of the best meals she could ever remember eating. That seemed to be happening every time she ate with this man.

15. The Drinking Game

The salad was delicious. The lasagna was to die for. The company was, well… it was also pretty good. They had finished dinner and were now moving into a big open room – twelve-foot ceilings, fireplace. Just more evidence to support Claire's theory of a fairy tale. Any moment now, she half expected John Wayne or Jimmy Stewart to walk through the front door and tip their hat to her.

Cole placed the whiskey she had brought and two glasses on the coffee table before moving to the fireplace. Claire sat on the couch, leather of course, and watched him build a fire. She tried not to stare at how his lovely bum fit so snuggly into his jeans. A few minutes later, she had no idea if she had failed or not at her attempt, but she felt flushed.

"The temp is supposed to drop again tonight," Cole said, standing and moving to sit on the couch. He wasn't exactly sitting right next to her, but he was close enough that she could smell that he had put on some sort of cologne. A deep musky smell. It suited him.

Claire realized he was looking at her somewhat expectantly and she realized she hadn't said a word since they had left the dining room. Throughout dinner, they had chatted like old friends, traded smiles, and had a grand old time. Now, she scrambled to say something that made sense. Something other than "your butt looks fantastic in those jeans".

"The dining room," she blurted before she had even thought about it. Cole raised his eyebrows and leaned forward, encouraging her to go on. Claire grasped at straws, thoughts sifting through her fingers like she was a six-year-old talking to her first crush. She lunged for the first question she could string together.

"How did you learn to place a setting like that?"

Cole chuckled, relaxed, and leaned back into the couch. "My grandma had a book, something about etiquette and what not. It was probably something of her mother's, the thing barely held together. She showed it to me when I was a boy. I'm sure I'd been sent into the house as punishment for something. But she fed me a plate of cookies and let me leaf through the book. Came in handy, eh?"

He looked at her expectantly.

"That's very," Claire searched for the right word, "sweet." She smiled at the cowboy and pictured a mini-him with cookie crumbs and bits of chocolate smeared all over his face. "I never knew my grandma."

Cole acted like he was going to touch her shoulder in comfort, but then stopped. "I'm sorry," was all he said, eyes moving toward the fire.

"Nothing to be sorry about. That's the way it goes sometimes." Claire didn't want the evening to be ruined with sad thoughts. She grabbed the bottle of whiskey. "Shall we play a drinking game?"

"A drinking game? You think you can hold your own against me?" The challenge in his eyes was unmistakable.

In response, Claire poured two healthy shots and handed him one. She lifted her own, ready to clink glasses. "May the better man win."

Cole's grin was impish and breathtaking. He clinked with her glass, and they both threw back the shots, and then they both stuttered a bit as the whiskey burned going down.

"That's damn fine whiskey." Cole placed his glass on the coffee table.

"Agreed." Claire placed her glass next to his and began to refill them both.

"Are we just going to take shot after shot?" he said with skepticism in his glance. "That doesn't seem like too much of a game to me."

Claire rolled her eyes at him as she put the whiskey bottle down. "Oh no. You don't get off that easy. That was just a warm-up shot. We are going to play two truths and a lie. Whoever doesn't guess correctly, takes a shot."

He grinned. "This isn't going to go well for you."

"You are far too cocky for your own good, Mister Patrick Cole."

"Let the games begin!" he crowed. "You first."

"I have written thirty-five books. I have never ridden a horse before this trip. I can cook your socks off."

Cole stared deep into her eyes. It made the whiskey in her belly light on fire.

"Come on," she said as she licked her lips. "I started you off with an easy one."

"Well, I know you ain't never rode a horse before Lady. That's pretty clear." He drummed his fingers on his knee. "Thirty-five books is a lot." Claire couldn't tell if he was pretending to give the game that much consideration or if he was just pulling her leg. "The books. That one is a lie."

Claire's mouth opened into a playful but shocked look. "How dare you!" She playfully slugged his arm. "I'll have you know that I've written thirty-five books, and twelve of them have been on the New York Times Best Seller list!" She handed him his shot of whiskey. "Drink up."

Cole rolled his eyes. "I guess I should have known, since you had a shopping basket full of canned ravioli this afternoon." He downed his shot and grimaced. "Or did I just want to let you win the first round?"

Claire slugged him on the arm again, harder this time. "Better not have. That would be a pretty crappy way to play."

"All right, all right," Cole raised his hand in defeat. "I just didn't think it through, okay? Maybe the first shot already went to my head."

"It will be a long night for you, then," she teased, trailing her fingertips down the bottle of top-shelf whiskey.

"My turn." Cole screwed his face in mock concentration. Claire made to slug his arm again. "Okay! Okay," he said. "Here goes. I could ride a horse before I could walk. I can cook your socks off," he gave her a meaningful stare before continuing, "and I won my first rodeo when I was fifteen."

Claire knew he could cook. That wasn't even a question. But the other two statements, she was having trouble deciphering which one was the lie. Finally, it clicked. "The rodeo. That one is a lie."

The look of surprise on Cole's face was immensely amusing. Claire gave him her most charming grin, held her hands under her chin, and batted her eyelashes at him. The shocked look slowly turned into a smile.

"How did you know?" he asked.

"If you had won a rodeo, you would have one of those giant belt buckles, and I bet you would never take it off!" Claire dissolved into laughter at the mental picture she had concocted for herself.

Cole laughed too. "I suppose you are right. Or at least, fifteen-year-old me would have. I would hope I have better taste now."

Claire gave him a skeptical look. But then she leaned forward, toward him. "My turn."

* * *

Though he was starting to feel light-headed, Cole found the evening delightful. Dinner had gone supremely well and this drinking game, well that was turning up all sorts of interesting information on his guest.

He now knew that her first celebrity crush was George Clooney, the ER version. She had always wanted to be a better cook but could burn boiling water. Her first kiss was in a janitor's closet in high school. Chad had asked her out with two dozen roses and a card. Her parents were both gone. She had been lonelier in the past six months that she ever wanted to admit.

The woman that had gotten stuck in that mud puddle was gone. Cole could see now the humanity of her, not just a dumb tourist he had to cater too. He had been a fool to ever think of her that way in the first place. He had been a fool about a lot of things over the years. His fuzzy mind didn't want to think about that right now. It wanted to think about the very tipsy, maybe even drunk, beautiful woman sitting next to him.

As the game had gone on, they had slid closer and closer to each other on the couch. It had been done on purpose, for Cole's part. Had it on hers? If her smile was any indication, it certainly had been.

"I love whiskey. I should be asleep right now. I think you are very handsome." The game was still on, and it was his turn to guess.

Cole leaned forward and looked very deeply into Claire's beautiful eyes. "Those are all very, very, true," he said gravely.

They seemed to lean in closer to each other, pulled by an unseen force neither of them could deny. Maybe gravity? Gravity wanted them to be together. Cole almost shuddered at the drunken thought.

Just when he thought that their lips would finally meet, Claire burst into a fit of laughter and fell against his chest. He smiled and put his arms around her. Even without a kiss, he would hold this woman as long as she would let him. It felt right, safe even.

He felt her relax and melt against him. "Why is your heart beating so fast?" she asked, voice muffled by his shirt.

Cole chuckled. "I have a high heart rate."

"It's not the whiskey?" she asked innocently, or not so innocently.

"No, sweetie," he said, stroking a strand of her hair behind her ear and leaving his hand on her shoulder.

They had both had too much whiskey, and he knew it. But that didn't stop the desire that was flooding his system. It didn't prevent his senses from being overwhelmed by the smell of the tourist's hair, the feeling of her body his arms, the sound of her voice so close to him.

"Mmmm," she purred and snuggled in closer to him. Cole thought he might burst with happiness. His crush was definitely deepening. He had to tell her, had to tell her how he felt. Guest/host rules be damned.

He sucked in a large breath, filling his lungs to bursting, ready to take the plunge. But just as he found the right words and herded them to the edge of his tongue, Claire shifted. She pulled back just enough to look directly into his eyes, hand on his chest. All of the air left his lungs, and he feared his heart might stop beating. Her beauty in the firelight was undeniable.

"I am sorry," she said softly, looking down, avoiding eye contact.

Cole reached out and tipped her chin up. Her skin felt so soft against his rough hands. He found it hard to move his gaze up from those perfect lips to her perfect eyes. This had to be the whiskey, right?

"You don't have anything to be sorry for," he told her, because at that moment, she really was perfect to him.

"No," she said softly, the word barely forming on her lips. "I was beastly to you yesterday. And you didn't deserve it."

He shook his head at her, still holding her chin. He couldn't make himself let go. Was that shame he could see in her eyes. It was unwarranted. The whiskey, the firelight, her in his arms, it made yesterday's tiff seem like an eon ago and unimportant. Cole let go of her chin and held the hand that was on his chest. He could feel how fast his heart was beating. It was not just that he had a rapid heartrate.

"No, no," she again said softly. "I, well, I came here to write a book. I lied to my editor and told her that it was almost completed. It's not. I hadn't even started it yet."

She pulled back further from him and started fidgeting. Cole just listened, sensing that was what she needed.

"I couldn't start. Every time I tried to get something down on the page, stupid Chad's face would appear in my head." A fire burned in her eyes. "That worthless cad ruined everything!"

Cole reached out and rubbed his hand on her arm. She had more muscle than he expected. Claire responded to his touch and leaned in against his chest again. She let out a long sigh.

"But I am finally making some headway. I think." She snuggled in closer, and Cole could feel her breath whispering against his neck. God, it felt good. "But that phone call I got yesterday? They want the first draft by the end of the week. And I don't know if I can do that."

Cole ran his hand up and down her back, trying to comfort her. He understood her distress. Hell, if anyone understood the pressure of creating something out of nothing, it was him. Mr. Foster certainly didn't.

He shook his head and banished all thoughts of Mr. Foster and the loan against the ranch. He wanted to be in the moment, here, with Claire.

"I know you can do it," he encouraged her, whispered into her hair. "You've written thirty-five books. Of course, you can write this one."

She snuggled in closer, and Cole hoped it meant he had said the right thing. She let out a sigh that tickled his neck. He tightened his arms around her.

"I got snippy with you, because," she started to admit. "Well, because of this." She raised her head just enough to place a light kiss at the base of his neck. To Cole, it felt like she lit a fire in his veins.

"You've distracted me. You and your stupid wood chopping," she growled. "But you've also helped me relax, feel like I can be myself again."

She paused, and Cole was afraid she wouldn't go on. And he needed her to go on, needed to hear those words falling from her lips as she ran her hand over his side.

"I shouldn't be so eager to jump into a summer fling, not right now," Claire whispered. Cole thought his heart might stop. "But I need it. I need this." Claire's words seemed to dance along the firelight, filling Cole with hope and desire.

His mind scrambled, a fuzzy whiskey-led scramble, for the words he wanted to say to her. How he had felt the same way. He didn't have time for a summer fling either. Yet, here they were, in each other's arms.

It seemed like it took an eternity for him to gather the right words for the woman in his arms. But finally, he felt sure about what he wanted to say.

"Claire," he said softly, reaching up to stroke her soft hair. She didn't respond, didn't move. "Claire?"

Cole angled his head to look down at her. Her eyes were closed, and her breathing was deep and even.

"I like you too," he sighed and wrapped his arms tightly around her, knowing she couldn't hear him from wherever she was in dreamland.

16. The Second Dinner

Claire woke up to discover that she was on the couch in the main house's living room. The fire had died out, and the sun was filtering in through the windows, it's beams playing with the dust flecks floating through the air. She groaned and stretched her body out from its curled up position. She had to jerk her hand out to save the heavy blanket that covered her from falling to the floor.

She sighed and pulled it back up to her chin, savoring the warmth and comfort it gave her. It reminded her of a different warmth and comfort she had felt the night before. All the whiskey had made things a little fuzzy, but she thought she might have apologized for being such an ass to the cowboy. And she defiantly remembered how it felt to kiss his neck.

Claire felt a smile grow slyly across her face. She closed her eyes and pictured what he had looked like with the firelight framing his face. Fires made everything more romantic, she noted. She was going to have to include that in a story somewhere along the line. Maybe in the book she should be working on in that very moment.

She heaved a sigh to pull herself back into the present, threw off the blanket, and stood up. That novel wasn't going to write itself. And since Cole wasn't around to hold her, she had better get to work. Claire giggled at the thought. Lord, she had it bad. Real bad.

Wandering into the kitchen, she found half a pot of coffee with a mug and a note placed next to it. The note read, "Dinner, again, tonight? 6 p.m. Enjoy the coffee. I think we will both need a little extra today."

Claire's smile grew wide. Come to think of it, she did have a little bit of a headache coming on. But it certainly wasn't the worst hangover she had ever experienced. She picked up the mug to fill it with coffee and discovered a small bottle of ibuprofen hiding behind it. "Good man," she whispered.

After pouring a mug of the delicious black liquid, she used it to wash down four of the coated pills. Probably not the best way to take painkillers, but probably not the worst, either, she mused. Now, to get some work done.

She picked up the coffee and, after slipping a few extra pills in her jeans pocket just in case, headed for her cabin. The sun was warm, and the fresh air pushed gently against her in a light breeze. It smelled like pine trees and dirt. Claire briefly looked around the ranch yard. Neither Buck nor Cole was in sight. I might actually get some work done, she thought, without that man to distract me. A sly grin filled her face again. She guessed she didn't entirely mind being distracted.

If she were going to have a summer fling. She might as well have a damn good one. But first, she needed to make some serious headway on her book.

* * *

Cole knocked on the guest cabin door. It was almost six, despite the sun still being fairly high in the blue sky. He loved this time of year when the days grew longer and the nights loosened their icy grip. Spring was never more of a rebirth than it was on a ranch.

He heard a few hurried footsteps and then watched the door fly open. Claire stood there, holding the door, her hair a mused mess, and still wearing the same clothes from the night before.

"It's not six yet, is it?" she said, casting a nervous glance down at her wrinkled shirt.

"No, not quite yet," Cole smiled. He held out a tiny white flower, which looked ridiculous in his large tan hands. "Buck wanted me to give this to you." Sure enough, Buck was sitting at his side, grinning, playing his part perfectly.

"Oh," Claire said, taking the flower and inhaling its fragrance. She dropped to one knee and reached out to scratch the dog's ears. "What a sweet gesture. It won't make an arm any less sore from throwing all of those tennis balls, though." She looked up at Cole and grinned. He couldn't help but smile back. Buck sat there, soaking up all the attention. He clearly thought he was the center of the universe.

Claire stood up and pulled at her t-shirt. "Let me just freshen up, and then I will be right back."

"Great. I thought we could maybe cook together tonight. It seems you could use the practice," Cole teased.

She shot him a look, and just as she started to push the wooden door closed, she stuck her tongue out at him. Then she was gone. Cole couldn't help the chuckle that broke out of his chest. He swore he heard her laughter answer his from the other side of the door.

A half hour later, she appeared in the kitchen doorway in a fresh set of clothes and with the tiny flower tucked into her hair. She was breathtaking. As always.

"Come on in," Cole said, gesturing with the avocado he was holding.

"Oh, why thank you," she trilled, crossing the threshold and making her way over to him. "Kind sir."

She stood next to him, glancing at all of the ingredients he had gathered on the counter. "And what is for dinner tonight?"

"Well, I thought we would start with something easy, due to your marvelous cooking skills."

She cut him off by slugging him on the shoulder.

"Hey!" He rubbed his arm as if it were a great wound. "And," he drew the word out, "because I am still nursing the tail end of a hangover." He caught her satisfied grin out of the corner of his eye. "Which is your fault too, by the way."

"Hey," she said, holding her hands up in surrender, "I didn't pour the whiskey down your throat."

Cole hummed a non-committal response and rolled his eyes. He picked up a knife and pointed to a package of ground beef. "You can start by browning that. Skillet's already on the stove." When she hesitated, he said, "You do know how to cook simple burger, don't you?"

"Ummm," was the only response he got as she stared down at the red meat. He couldn't help but chuckle.

"Okay, okay." He herded her toward the stove, carrying the meat for her. He positioned her right in front of the burner and pointed toward the nob. "Turn the head up to medium-high, and then dump the meat in the skillet."

Cole didn't stay by her side while she completed the task.

He wandered over to the pantry and pulled out an apron. He walked back over, and as Claire turned to him, he plopped it down over her head. She looked down and studied it.

"Why don't I get huge boobs like yours?" she asked, acting offended.

"Because you already have perfect boobs." The words were out of his mouth so fast he couldn't stop them. He watched Claire's mouth pop open in a surprised little "O", and then felt a blush rush to his face. He turned away and stalked over to where the other ingredients waited.

"We are having tacos," he said gruffly, back to his guest. "The meat is the most important part. Don't mess it up."

"Oh?" her voice had definitely taken on a tone of merriment.

"Just stir it every once in a while, to make sure it all gets cooked." Cole tried not to bark out the words, but his embarrassment might have gotten the better of him.

"Whatever you say, boss," Claire said, and he could hear the smile in her voice.

The rest of the dinner prep went according to plan. Claire did not burn the meat and Cole didn't make any more foolish comments. Thank the good Lord for small miracles. They sat in the dining room again, no candlesticks this time.

"Can we avoid the whiskey tonight?" Claire asked, her face the picture of innocence. Cole knew better.

"I hope so," he answered. "I'm getting too old to drink like that. In fact, I don't think I've ever drank like that."

Happiness twinkled in her eyes. "Good. I got a decent amount of work done today. But I bet it would have been even more if I hadn't been nursing that hangover."

"I can relate to that." Cole raised his glass of water in a toast. They watched each other over the tops of their glasses as they drank. He was irresistibly drawn to her. To everything about her – her voice, her eyes, her mouth, her wit. He needed to tell her, and not when she was passed out like she had the night before.

"I think I'm going to try and hold off my editor for a while longer," she continued around a bite of a taco. "I think I am really onto something. If I have a little more time, I could make it into something great. I'm sure of it."

"That's wonderful. I'm glad you've found some inspiration out here."

"Yes, inspiration," she mused, looking at him with half-hooded eyes.

The air was suddenly charged with electricity. Inspiration or no, there was something between them. Cole was sure that if he just reached out and touched her, they would lose themselves to it. They stared intensely into each other's eyes, no longer caring about the carefully made tacos. This is it, Cole thought. This is my chance. He broke her gaze, just for a moment, and took a deep breath.

"I, ah," Claire's words came out in a sudden rush. "I've never had tacos as good as these. Chad could never make them as good."

And just like that, the moment was gone. No man wanted to profess his attraction to a woman after the dreaded ex had just entered the conversation.

"I, umm," he grasped at straws for something to say, "I'm glad you like them. You did a good job with the taco meat." He tried to steer the conversation away from her ex, Chad. But an awkward silence developed between them. Gone was the witty banter and flirting. Now, the room just felt stale.

"That was the wrong thing to say," Claire said, setting down a half-eaten taco on her plate. Her eyes told him that she had felt the climate of the room change too. If he had any kind of balls, he would tell her anyway. He would be able to bring the conversation back around. But he was too busy beating the daylights out of this mythical Chad guy, in his mind.

The silence drew out longer than Cole meant it to. Claire suddenly stood up.

"You know," she said, backing toward the kitchen, "I think I just came up with something I need to add to my manuscript."

She had reached the kitchen doorway, and Cole was barely able to pull himself out of his mind to listen to what she was saying.

"I have to go work on it," she gave him a half-apologetic smile, but also looked relieved to be making an escape. "Inspiration's whim and all."

And with that, she was gone. Cole was alone in the dining room with a plate of tacos sitting in front of him.

That was it. That was the moment he had been waiting for. It had been perfect. And he had blown it. Blown it hard.

"Damn," he cursed and got up to clear the dishes.

17. The Editor's Email

Despite having written a few hundred more words after dinner the night before, Claire was up with the sun the next morning, her fingers clacking away, hoping magic was pouring into her keyboard. She hadn't really lied to the cowboy. Claire had definitely found inspiration here, in the magnificent mountains and landscapes of Montana. This novel was going to be some of her best work yet, and she knew it. So did it really matter if it was more than just the mountains inspiring her? Her characters and plot flew down onto page after page, filling her novel and head with ideas and pictures that made her muse take flight.

Sure, she had squandered several months weeping over a dumb-ass love affair that hadn't worked out. But this was her greatest work to date! It deserved to be the best. She only needed a little more time. Nervously, Claire tried to stay on track, but in the back of her mind, she started to rehearse the magic words that she hoped would sway the publishing house.

As if on cue, her cell phone dinged a notification at her. Claire finished up the paragraph she was working on, then stood and stretched out her limbs, groaning as the tightness eased. It was only the second or third time she had left the chair that day, and it had to be mid-afternoon by now. Having satisfied her stiff muscles, she walked over to the nightstand and picked up her phone.

Sure enough, she had a new email, and it was from her editor. A flash of worry hit Claire, but she quickly pushed it away. She thumbed to her main screen and tapped on the email app. Nothing happened. She tapped again, with a little more aggression. Still, nothing. The screen didn't change. Then Claire realized she didn't have enough cell signal to download the email.

Grumbling about the cursed wilderness, she crawled into the one corner of the cabin that had an almost decent amount of cell signal. She couldn't help but laugh at herself as she held the phone far above her head while the email downloaded. "Desperate times," she muttered while desperately hoping it wasn't actually a desperate time. Not yet anyway.

She was halfway done thinking through her next chapter when the phone chimed again. Download complete, Claire thought triumphantly. Good thing too – her arm wasn't going to take much more of being hoisted in the air. It had endured too much abuse from all fetch with that adorable blue heeler.

Thumbing to the email, Claire's eyes quickly scanned the words her editor had written. It was a basic demand for an update. Oh, Claire thought, for pity's sake. Though, she supposed she had never been in this position before. She had always met her deadlines previous to stupid Chad. But then again, she had been stringing the publishing company along for months now. All thoughts and ideas of asking for more time fled her mind like children running from nap time.

Panic and anxiety bloomed in Claire's chest. She really, really needed to get them something, and quick. Something that would reassure them that she was truly getting some outstanding work done. Her mind scrambled. Maybe if she buckled down and got them the first draft, she would have time to go back later and fix it up, make it as good as she knew it could be.

She forced her body to take longer, slower breaths. The panic started to abate.

"Yes," Claire told the room. "That is what I will do."

All the distractions would need to be cut out. No more fetch in the morning, no more dinners, no more whiskey drinking games or dancing in the firelight. Not until the book was done. It was the start of a plan, anyway. She could do this; she had to do this. She didn't have a choice.

Her attention zeroed in on her phone as she quickly, with two thumbs, typed out a response to her editor. She claimed, honestly, that she didn't have enough cell service to send the chapters she had done, but would drive into town in the next couple of days to send them out.

As she hit the send button, her tunnel vision faded just enough for a dull thud sound to reach her ears. She could identify that sound now. It was Cole chopping firewood. And if she had to bet, she would say he was probably shirtless. Or at the very least had his shirt unbuttoned. It was a lovely spring day, after all. Maybe she could spare a minute from her work, but only a minute. A quick break might help her focus, after all. It was only natural.

She stepped out onto the porch, the sun lovingly caressing her face and bare arms. Claire sighed and breathed in deeply. The air smelled warm and like new spring wildflowers. It smelled like hope. Despite her urgent need to get her book done and off to the publisher, she felt a little seed of peace and happiness take root in her chest. It was a new feeling. If this kind of situation had happened with any of her other books, she would have been freaking out and keeping up a steady stream of coffee, or booze, depending on the hour of the day.

The dull thud of ax meeting wood rang out again. It pulled at her like a magnet. She smiled and answered the pull. Yes, it was some sort of happiness that seemed to finally be blooming in her.

Buck trotted up to her as soon as he spied her coming toward the corral. His happy little grin was always a permanent fixture on his face, it would seem. She crouched down and held his face before scratching behind his ears. "Such a good puppy," she murmured, spoiling the dog with her attention.

"Not that good," a dark voice answered from a few feet away.

"Oh?" Her voice and eyebrow raised in question. She took in the sight of Cole. No shirt, lean and muscled body gleaming in the warm sun. A shiver raced up her spine at the beautiful sight, and Claire had to fight to keep a school-girl grin from betraying her thoughts.

"That little sucker decided not to catch the mouse that has taken up residence in the main house." Playful irritation graced Cole's voice as he half leaned on his ax, staring down his dog. A dog who was apparently unconcerned with the scolding and continued to grin between the two humans.

"Ummm," Claire hummed. "Isn't that a job for a cat?" A light laugh twinkled at the end of her question as the breeze pushed at her hair. She felt so alive here with Cole. There was no denying it. Even if the man was confused about the roles that cats and dogs played in the real world.

"Stupid dog is better than a cat." Cole grinned as if he knew he sounded absurd. "But not today," he raised his voice with the last few words and glared at the blue heeler.

"Why do you have mice in the spring anyway?" Claire couldn't help but ask, her curiosity getting the better of her. As it always did.

"Lord only knows," was the answer. "Perhaps they wanted some of that good cooking we've been doing the last few nights."

"Fair enough."

A silence developed as the two gazed at each other. An open hunger seemed to alight both of their eyes. Damn, Claire thought, we can't go on like this much longer. Something has to break.

"Can I help?" she finally asked, desperate to draw the heat of the cowboy's gaze away from her.

"Have you ever split wood before?" he teased, giving her an appraising look.

"You know perfectly well that I have not," she countered. "But I am a quick learner."

"Oh!" Cole exaggerated the word, big and drawn out. "In that case, we'd better start you off with just carrying the wood."

"Fine." Claire rolled her eyes. Buck yipped, not happy that he was no longer the center of attention.

"Okay," Cole beckoned her closer to him with a crooked finger. When she was close enough, he reached for her arms, which were still hanging at her sides. She didn't resist him as his gloved hands slid up her arms, moving them out in front of her.

"You want to stack the wood on your arms like this," he said, his hands not releasing her arms. She found his grip reassuring and solid. In fact, she had trouble focusing on his words, but forced herself to pay more attention. Until she looked into his eyes, that is. Damn. She could lose herself in those eyes if she allowed herself to.

The cowboy moved his hands, slowly releasing her arms. Her eyes broke from his, embarrassment flooding her system as she realized she had licked her lips while she had been staring into those deep pool-like eyes of his. But she caught a grin playing across his face and returned it. Hell, if he didn't already know how attracted she was to him, he was some kind of fool.

Cole reached down and picked up the pieces of the last log he had split. He placed them gently in her waiting arms. The wood felt rough and grainy, but it smelled amazing. Like Christmas, only fresher. The wood wasn't as heavy as she expected, but then again, there were only three pieces.

"Carry it like this," Cole said gently. The soundwaves of his voice washed over Claire in the most delicious way. "As you get stronger, you'll be able to carry more."

She liked the way he said that, as if she would be here for a long, long time. Even though she knew it couldn't be, it was nice to dream.

"Where am I taking this?" she asked, trying not to let the daydream sweep her away completely.

"Into the house," Cole said, lifting the ax and placing another log on the chopping block. "I was going to fill that spot next to the fireplace and then do a little extra for your cabin." He looked her up and down. "You don't have to help, you know. You're the guest here, after all."

"I'd like to help," Claire said, looking up at him through her lashes. "Besides, I need the distraction. I'll write better if I take a short break."

"As you wish," Cole said, placing a new log on the chopping block. Claire wondered if he knew he was quoting *The Princess*

Bride. "Just take care not to get any slivers in those arms."

Claire nodded, and he turned back to his task. She couldn't help but watch as he lifted the ax, the muscles in his back tightening and moving. It was a work of art.

The sound of the wood splitting brought her out of her head, and she headed toward the house with her armful of wood. Several trips later, the cache in the house was full, and they started on the guest cabin. They didn't talk too much more, just a few words here or there. The silence felt easy, right, and comfortable.

It didn't take long before the chore was done. The cowboy and guest stood awkwardly in the yard, facing each other. Neither quite willing to break off the connection. Finally, Claire did. She knew she had too much work to do to stand there gawking at her host.

"I," she started, fumbling over her words slightly. "I have to get back to work."

Cole nodded, not saying anything, but she did notice his body tense up.

"I'm already behind," she continued, feeling the need to explain. "And the publisher is breathing down my neck."

"You'll get it done," Cole said softly, looking down and not meeting her eye as he said the words. His work boot scuffed at some invisible thing in the dirt. "I have faith in you."

Claire let out a merry laugh. "Why, thank you, kind sir." She gave him the brightest smile. "Between you and Buck, I'm sure I have all the support I need to get the job done."

To her surprise, Claire found that she truly meant the words. It wasn't just the mountain air, or the spring flowers, or the dashing cowboy, it was all of it combined. Inspiration wasn't the right word. Comfortable was closer, but still not quite right. With all the thousands upon thousands of words she had written over the years, she couldn't quite find the right ones to describe the feeling building inside of her.

"It will be a great book," he said quietly, as he turned toward the barn.

"Thank you," Claire said just as softly, turning toward the guest cabin.

It was like they both knew that if they didn't move apart, they would inevitability get much, much closer. And then, who knew what would happen. Well, Claire could imagine what could happen. That was a fact. She hummed a little tune to herself as she walked back into her cabin.

Sitting down at her laptop, the characters came to life through Claire's fingers. Publishers be damned, this was going to be the best book she had written. And she had all of Paradise Valley Ranch to thank for it.

18. The First Kiss

A soft knock echoed through the cabin and Claire barely pulled her head out of her work long enough to call a mumbled "Come in," before furiously typing away at yet another paragraph. Wholly and utterly absorbed in her work, she didn't even bother to take note of who had entered the cabin, until a wet, slimy tongue began pushing against her toes. Her foot pushed the dog away as she typed out the last few words of her thought and then leaned back in her chair.

Claire stretched out her cramped muscles and groaned, looking down at the blue heeler, who joined her with a stretch of his own – his front paws out before him, head pushed down – and a giant yawn. She reached out a hand to scratch under the pup's chin.

"What are you doing here, buddy?" she asked in a ridiculous voice people used for dogs and babies.

The dog's eyes rolled in happiness toward the door, and Claire suddenly realized there had, indeed, been an actual knock. One that a dog couldn't have achieved on his own. Sure enough, a certain cowboy was darkening her doorstep. A slow smile slid across her face, and she neglected the dog to stand.

"Well, hello there," she said, almost shyly. Why she felt shy all of a sudden, only the Lord knew. Maybe it was the scene she had been writing, or maybe it was just it was the butterflies that appeared in her stomach every time she saw the man.

His grin lit up the whole room. As he took a step over the cabin threshold, Claire realized he was holding a tray with the most delicious looking food, complete with a vase and a single flower. The butterflies in her stomach went mad, utterly mad.

Cole glanced around the room and apparently didn't find what he was looking for, because he said, "Let's go to the front porch on the main house. There is a little table out there, so you don't have to eat dinner on your bed." There was a twinkle in his eye at that last word.

The butterflies in her stomach seemed to sigh and flutter away. She almost had the nerve to feel abandoned by them. Almost. But she grinned at the cowboy anyway.

Claire followed Cole and Buck as they crossed the distance between the guest cabin and the main house. Dusk was upon the ranch yard, coating everything in a beautiful golden yellow. The songbirds were serenading the enchanted world Claire found herself in, and she loved it. The view of following her cowboy host wasn't bad either. It was a real pity more men didn't wear Wranglers.

They stepped up onto the wraparound porch, and Cole set the dinner tray down on a small table in between two rocking chairs. "Dig in," he said, gesturing to one of the chairs, a sly smile spread across his face.

Damn, those dimples, was all that ran through Claire's mind.

Buck nosing at the tray of food distracted her long enough to break her concentration away from her dashing host. Dinner on a tray, with a flower – this was the stuff novels were made of, certainly not real life. Never her real life, anyway.

"I hope you don't mind Mexican," Cole commented, taking his own seat across from her. "It's the easiest thing for me to make, being that I typically have most of the ingredients on hand."

Claire picked up a fork and dug into the plate of food. "I'm sure it's just fine."

She took a bite, and the flavor exploded in her mouth. Raising her eyebrows at the man she exclaimed, "This is better than fine. Holy cow!"

Cole chuckled and leaned back in his rocking chair, setting a leisurely pace. Buck appeared out of nowhere with a bone in his jaws – Claire hadn't even realized he was gone – and plopped down at their feet. His teeth grated against the hard surface of the bone, his tail constantly wagging. The dog seemed content, and Claire discovered she was too.

"We had an old hand who used to cook sometimes. He taught me what he knew, saying his grandmother taught him," Cole explained, his hands crossed over his stomach as he rocked. He looked comfortable, at ease, perfectly happy with the enchanted world of his ranch. Claire envied him and admired him too. "Old José went back to Mexico to help with his son's new spread. Never heard from him again. But if I know him at all, I bet he is making enchiladas, just like those," he nodded toward Claire's plate, which was half demolished, "for all the ranch hands he can find."

"Well," Claire mused, "should you ever hear from him again, you will have to thank him for me. This is amazing! I will never be able to order enchiladas at a restaurant again. They don't even come close to being as delicious as these." She shoveled another bite into her mouth, wondering if it was because she hadn't eaten for most of the day, or because of the company, or because she was making some headway on her novel, but the food was truly wonderful.

They fell into a comfortable silence, rocking, looking out across the countryside. It feels right and good to be here, in this moment, Claire thought. She wanted to say so, but couldn't find the right words. She didn't want to give Cole the "wrong impression," but it wasn't really wrong. Everything about this felt romantic – the sunset, the ranch, him, all of it. She could stay here forever.

Finishing off her plate with a satisfied mumble of appreciation, she looked up to catch her host staring at her. Maybe staring was the wrong word – looking her over, perhaps. She straightened in her chair but found herself staring back. And she really was staring, she could admit that to herself. She longed to feel his arms around her again like they had been when they danced in the starlight, or when he was showing her how to cook in the kitchen. Claire inhaled deeply, almost able to smell his heady scent – sweat, wood, and earth. It was intoxicating, to be sure.

"It sure is lovely tonight," Cole said, not taking his eyes off of her. Claire desperately wanted to know if he really meant the evening in a general sense, or her. Oh, how badly she wanted it to be her.

"It sure is," she responded, also not taking her eyes off of him, because it was him, himself, that she was referring to. The dashing cowboy that was turning her life upside down and inside out. How was she ever going to go back to the city after this?

To distract herself from the question, she stood up abruptly and picked up the tray. "I'll clean this up real quick."

Cole jumped up just as fast. "You don't have to do that," he said, reaching for the tray.

Claire held the tray closer to herself and took a step back from him. "Nonsense," she huffed. "You cooked. The least I can do is carry the tray inside. Sit back down." She nodded to his abandoned chair, which was still rocking from his abrupt departure. "I'll be right back." She winked at him as she turned and headed to the kitchen with the tray.

When she came back to the porch with two steaming mugs of coffee in hand, she found Cole rocking gently with his eyes closed. There was a small smile on his face like he was perfectly contented. Claire cleared her throat, and he opened his eyes to look up at her with a playfully weary look on his face.

"I was worried that you had died in there or something," he drawled out. Buck lifted his head from its resting place on his front paws to confirm the suspicion. "I was about to come in after you."

"Sure," Claire scoffed but held out a cup to him. "Looked like you were more interested in taking a nap."

"Maybe," Cole admitted, taking the mug from her hand. Their fingers brushed and lingered for far longer than was necessary. Claire prayed the shiver that ran up her spine didn't visibly manifest itself. Because that would have been utter foolishness and nonsense. She was only handing him a cup of coffee! Nothing to get so excited about.

Cole raised his eyebrows at her, and she rushed forward with the first words that popped into her head as she stepped toward her empty rocking chair. "Don't worry, it's decaf. You can go back to your nap anytime you please."

The cowboy let loose a jolly laugh, and Claire couldn't help but smile as she took a seat. She held the mug close to her face and savored the warmth and comfort she found there. It also gave her the perfect opportunity to stealthily take in the sight of her handsome host. Though it probably wasn't really all that stealthy, she supposed, since he was staring right back at her. There was entirely too much staring going on, Claire told herself – this would never work in one of my novels; I'd lose readers left and right.

"I appreciate the consideration of my sleep schedule, but I find I am much more willing to enjoy your company than take a nap at this present moment." Cole grinned and took a sip of the coffee. "Mmmm, this is good," he said appreciatively, the warmth of the slowly fading sun lighting his face in a golden wash.

Claire could only smile in return and sip at her own mug. She relaxed into her chair, just enjoying the general splendor of it all, her muscles loose and content after hours of being cramped up in her cabin. And then, like a tiny ant on the back of her brain, she could feel her work trying to get her attention. There was so much of it to be done, but the evening was so lovely. Claire decided she would give herself ten more minutes of luxury.

"Do you have a watch on?" she asked her cowboy host, who seemed to be watching her out of the corner of his eye.

"Sure do," he answered casually and then leaned forward to look into her eyes. "It's 7:37. Got a hot date or something?" Claire couldn't decide if that was a tinge of jealousy that edged the man's voice or not. She put on a teasing smile anyway.

"Maybe," she let the silence fill up the space between them for several seconds before continuing. "I have to get back to work, but I can't seem to make myself move. So ten more minutes, if you please." She nodded toward his wrist.

"As my lady commands," Cole said, leaning back in the rocking chair again and setting a slow but steady pace.

"My lady," Claire mused. "Commands. I rather like those words together." She watched the smile on his face as she slid her eyes closed, content to be in his calming presence. Content with her life as it was now, in the mountains of Montana, a fixture on Paradise Valley Ranch. She didn't want it to end.

Claire pushed all thoughts of her inevitable departure away. She didn't want to live in the past; stupid Chad had marred every part of that for her. Claire didn't want to live in the future either; the thought of going back to the city was heartbreaking. She was determined to live in the moment, perhaps for the first time in her life. Claire wasn't going to look forward or backward.

She slowly fluttered her eyes open and glanced at the cowboy. No, she was going to live right here, in this moment, for as long as she could. The small smile she had on her face, it turned into a grin. Cole grinned right back.

"It's one of those perfect kinds of evenings, isn't it?" he asked softly. Buck perked up his ears as if to hear more clearly.

"Yes," she answered, almost purring. "It is."

"I regret to tell you," he glanced down at his watch, "that your requested ten minutes are up." He looked back up into her eyes, and she saw something she couldn't quite read there.

Claire sighed heavily, deeply regretting her idea of ten more minutes. But even with living in the moment, her work still called to her. Now instead of an annoying ant, it had started to sound like a whole hive of yellow jackets in her head. Her body almost shuddered at the thought and protested as she stood up.

In two gulps, she downed the rest of her coffee. Cole stood and did the same.

"I have things I should get done as well," he told her.

"Oh really?" Claire said in a teasing voice as she put her mug down on the small table. "How could you? I've already helped with all of your chores."

Cole set his empty mug down next to hers. "While that may be true," he took a small step toward her, "there is still a lot more to be done to keep this place afloat. Maybe even more than I can do." A shadow passed across his face as he surveyed the ranch yard. Claire stepped closer and put a hand on his well-muscled arm.

"You'll find a way," she reassured him, taking yet another small step toward him. It was like a magnetic pull and she couldn't or wouldn't resist. "You will find a way to save this amazing ranch. I just know it."

The cowboy turned his head, and his eyes found hers, looking deeply into them. Claire saw a vulnerability, a pleading, a hope there that she had never seen in any other man's eyes. It was a beautiful thing, and she couldn't help but want to comfort him. She reached up and placed her hand gently on the side of his face as he turned to look away, making sure his eyes stayed with hers.

"You will, Patrick Cole," she whispered. "I promise, you will find a way."

And just like that, she felt heat traveling up her arm and realized what she was doing. She became conscious of the mere inches between their bodies, the warmth of the cowboy's skin, the smell of his body. Her own body froze, unwilling to back away, even as his hands went to her waist. Her mind was spinning about a thousand miles a minute. There was such heat in his eyes, she surely thought she would melt as her own arms encircled the cowboy's neck. She had never felt anything like this before. Not with stupid Chad, not with anyone. Ever.

Cole moved in even closer, their bodies pushing against one another. Heat spread all throughout Claire, and she leaned into it. When he moved to put his hand against her cheek, she thought her heart might explode from beating so fast.

This isn't happening, this isn't happening, her mind repeated over and over, even as the cowboy leaned his head down closer to hers. It felt like her lungs were going to seize up, even as her mind spun out of control.

And then his lips brushed against hers. Claire's mind suddenly imploded into silence, and there was only him and her. Nothing else. No books, no ranches that needed saving, no dogs, no past relationships. Just Claire and her cowboy.

She reached up hungrily and gripped at his short hair, forcing him into a real kiss, not just some innocent lip brushing. A small groan escaped the man as he pressed his lips more firmly into hers. Claire involuntarily answered in kind. She let her teeth nip at his lips and felt him shudder with pleasure.

Their arms were entangled now, holding on like there wasn't going to be a tomorrow. As far as Claire was concerned, there wasn't. Just as she felt his tongue running along her lip, she thought she heard the distant sound of a dog barking. She tried to brush it aside, only wanting more and more of Cole and his hands traveling up and down her back.

But then the sound of a vehicle door slamming broke the spell, and Cole pulled back. He didn't take his eyes from her and only stepped back enough that their bodies were no longer melded together as one. They were both panting and had ridiculous grins plastered on their faces.

"Pardon the interruption," a gruff voice said, accompanying uneven footsteps on the gravel drive.

Claire glanced over and stepped back from Cole. An older man in blue jeans and a plaid shirt was walking up the front step with the help of a cane.

"Cole," he said, after glancing between the two newly minted lovers and leaning down heavily on his cane. "We need to talk."

19. The End of the Ranch

Cole watched Claire walk back across the yard to her guest cabin. He swore she was reluctant in doing so, looking back over her shoulder several times. It took every ounce of grit and good sense in him to not run after her and pull her back into his arms. Kissing her, well, kissing her felt like finally coming home, after all this time.

A throat cleared and Cole forced himself to turn to the old man that now stood on his porch. He knew the man. Had known him for years, in fact. Cole cleared his throat and held out his hand in greeting.

"Evening, Chuck." The old man's grip was as firm and as solid as ever, which was not surprising in the least. "How can I help you this evening?"

Chuck let go of Cole's hand and turned toward the house. "Let's go inside. My old bones quiet down when I'm sitting in a comfortable chair. As I remember, you have one or two of those."

Cole let him lead the way; Chuck knew the house just as well as he did. As they walked into the living room, the old man pointed to the bottle of whiskey that still sat on the coffee table. "Wouldn't mind a hit of that," he said as he settled his small but formidable frame into a large wingback chair. "In fact, we will probably both need it."

Cole tore himself away from the memories that the whiskey and shot glasses evoked, memories of Claire and the firelight making her hair glow, to focus on the words Chuck had said. It took him a couple of seconds, at which the old man raised his eyebrows, but he finally responded with a "Yes, sir. I do believe you are right," and headed off to the kitchen to get clean glasses and ice. It seemed like the occasion where one should sip at the whiskey, on the rocks. Which worried him, a little. It wasn't a good sign.

By the time he returned to the living room, Chuck had several papers laid out on the coffee table. Cole's stomach dropped. Not a good sign at all. He calmly tried to pour the whiskey, praying that his shaking hand wasn't too noticeable. He handed a glass of the amber liquid to the old man and made himself slowly sit down on the couch across from him.

"Thank you, son," Chuck said as he raised the glass in a salute before taking a deep sip. Then he set his face in a hard mask. Cole had seen this happen a time or two in the past, and his stomach went from dropping to turning into a boulder. He felt it pulling him down, trying to drown him.

"I've known your family for a long time," Chuck started out. Cole could only nod his agreement as he gripped his glass. "And I've watched over the legal affairs of this ranch even longer. I miss your granddaddy." He paused and looked right into Cole's eyes. "I know you do as well.

"He worked this land his whole life. Worked it hard, worked it well. He made something of it. But now, well, we all know what your father did, how he ruined it all. Stole the dream right out from under you. Made you clean up after his mess like the piece of shit he is."

Cole sat, unable to breathe, numb to speech. He knew all the words, had heard them before, too many times. He could probably recite the speech himself, but he couldn't. There could only be one of two reasons the old family attorney would make a visit out to Paradise Valley.

"I've been combing over everything, every document, every idea, good and bad, for months now," the attorney sighed. It seemed to deflate his frame. "I thought for sure I could find some kind of loophole or some way out of this mess."

Cole had been staring into his glass, but now he dared to look up into the eyes of the old man. He did not like the defeat he saw there. His throat tightened, and he fought back a small, or not so small, amount of panic.

"I cannot find a way to save this ranch," Chuck said, regret making his voice sound sad and maybe even heartbroken. "I tried. Damn me, I tried."

The old man drank the rest of his whiskey in one long draught and held the glass out for a refill. "I'm sorry, Patrick. I'm so sorry."

Cole nodded as he refilled the glass, not quite able to make his tongue form any words. He threw back his own whiskey and refilled his glass, taking another hit of the amber liquid before clearing his throat.

"I appreciate it, sir," he said around the tightness that threatened to cut off his ability to speak. The whiskey felt like it was curdling in his stomach. "I know you did everything you could.

My granddad would have been grateful. And you know I'm grateful."

His mind spun with a dozen ideas of how to make money quick, how to save his lively-hood, his family land, his life. But he knew it was no use, he would have to give it up, he would have to give everything up.

The old attorney nodded and took a sip from his glass of whiskey. "I think it would be best to put it up for sale, rather than let the bank call in the loan."

Cole nodded. There was no way he wanted his land to fall into the hands of that old creep, Mr. Foster. He would rather give the land to the devil himself.

"If you put it up now," Chuck continued, "perhaps one of those rich tourist folks will take interest over the summer. Pay a hefty price for such a beautiful view of the mountains. Then, well, then you could maybe sell it at a high enough price to have some seed money. Something to start over with."

The old man leaned back in his chair, resigned to defeat, and sipped at his whiskey while studying Cole. Cole was struggling to control his emotions. Selling the ranch would be like cutting off his right arm, but he knew it was the best thing. No, it was the only thing he could do. Even though the thought made him sick.

He threw back his glass of whiskey and poured another, hoping the burn would distract him. "I'll go into town in the morning and see Linda," he said, staring at the floor. Chuck grunted in agreement. "She sold a couple of big spreads out Big Sky way over the last few years. I suppose she would know best how to go about this."

"I think that is a good idea, son." The compassion in the man's eyes was almost too much for Cole to handle, and he went back to studying his glass. "Maybe you can go off into the sunset and have a nice life with that pretty little lady that was out front."

Cole's head jerked up at the words, and this time when he met the old man's eyes, teasing and merriment were peeking out from behind the compassion. "She's a guest, staying in grandma's old cabin."

"A guest..." Chuck's words trailed off into a chuckle. "Seemed a mite more than simple hospitality I saw when I drove up. Or is that how you treat all guests out here these days?"

Cole could only smile at the old family friend. He couldn't defend himself, had no right to. He had been caught red-handed.

"She is a pretty little thing," Chuck continued. "What's she doing out here, anyway?"

"She's a writer type, from the big city. Came out for some peace and quiet to finish up a manuscript, I believe."

Chuck laughed heartily and then said, "Is that what you kids call it these days? Back in my day, we used to call that necking." He laughed again and slapped his knee. Cole tried to hide the grin that suddenly lit up his face – tried and failed miserably.

"You really like her, don't you?" Chuck studied the cowboy's face carefully.

"Yeah," Cole drawled, playing with the glass in his hand and not meeting Chuck's eye. "I suppose I do. Nothing to be done about it though. She will leave in a few days, and I wouldn't have a thing to offer such a lady. Not now, anyway." He nodded toward the papers on the coffee table.

The pain of losing the ranch squeezed at his heart, threatening to overwhelm him. The pain of knowing he couldn't be with Claire, not really, not in the way he would want, was there too. All that pain seemed muddled into a big messy ball, sitting in the middle of his chest. He sighed and tried not to let his racing mind overwhelm him.

"Well," Chuck also drawled the word. "If you want my advice, and I'm not saying you do, but I'm an old man, so you have to humor me and listen anyway. I say you win the girl over and start a new life together."

Cole looked at the old man like he was crazy. Or from a different planet. Or just plain crazy.

"What?" Chuck said, shrugging. "It's a good plan."

"I'm going to put my only valuable in the whole world, my family's land, up for sale tomorrow, and you think some highfalutin city girl is going to want to run away with me?" Cole couldn't help how his voice raised in those last few words. It was the stupidest idea he had ever heard, and it wasn't just the whiskey burning in his belly that told him so.

"She didn't seem to care much for anything but you." The old man had a sly smile on his face, not deterred in the least by Cole's speech. "That is, from what I could tell when I drove up."

Cole rolled his eyes. He couldn't help it.

"Now, you listen here, son," Chuck leaned forward, a serious expression on his face. "Life is shorter than you think it is. Trust me, I would know. When you find someone you even remotely think you could love for the rest of your life, you hold on for dear life. My Matilda would tell you the same thing if she were still here." Tears glistened in the attorney's eyes. "We didn't think we could suit each other either. But we made it work because we knew that our lives would be sorry and lonely without one another. We were married for sixty-five years. And I miss her every second of every day."

Chuck let the words weigh heavy in the silent air, longer than Cole was really comfortable with. He was sure he saw a tear or two slip down the old man's face. He looked away, trying to be polite.

"Those were different times," Cole said softly, placing his glass on the table next to the whiskey bottle. "There was a war on."

"The times were no different!" Chuck practically shouted the words, surprising Cole with their venom. "Pull your head out of your ass, young Patrick Cole. Life is short. Get over yourself and your pride and see what is right in front of your eyes."

* * *

For the rest of the night, Cole couldn't get Chuck's words out his head, nor the look of undying devotion to his dead wife. It pulled at Cole in a way he couldn't explain. He had never felt anything like it. Sure, Claire was spunky, beautiful, independent, but was she the woman he wanted to run away with? Hell, he was still trying to wrap his head around the idea of having to run away in the first place. And, yes, that is precisely what selling the ranch felt like – running away.

Chuck stayed for a few hours, going over the logistics of selling and what Cole's legal responsibilities were. When they were finally settled on a plan, the moon had risen high in the sky, and the level of whiskey left in the bottle had gone down. As the taillights of the old attorney's vehicle faded down the driveway, Cole found himself glancing at the guest cabin.

The lights were still on, and he thought he could make out a faint outline of Claire. She was probably still working. He hoped she was having success with her manuscript. That's why she had come out here, after all. Even if it meant that she would be leaving as soon as it was done.

"Not that it matters now," Cole told Buck, who was sitting at his feet on the porch. "We will be leaving soon too."

He sighed and rubbed his forehead with one hand. The memory of the kiss they had shared lit a small flame in his belly. Comfort like that would be a beautiful thing at a time like this when his life felt like it was falling apart. But he couldn't ask Claire for that, she didn't owe him anything. She was his guest and could be nothing more.

Cole turned and walked into the cold, dark house, calling Buck to follow him. The dog seemed reluctant to go and kept glancing between the guest cabin and the cowboy.

"It's no use," Cole told him, not sure if he was talking about the girl or the ranch. "Let's go to bed."

20. The Phone Call

Claire worked all through the night. The words seemed to flow faster and with more certainty than they ever had before. Her hands flew across her keyboard, knowing that there was a light at the end of this very, very long tunnel. By the time the sun had started to lighten the sky from black to a gray-blue, Claire was absolutely buzzing with her success.

She stood up to make another pot of coffee. One more push, that was all she needed. One more chapter and the manuscript would be ready to send off to the publishing house, the first draft at least. Boy, would they ever be surprised. But hey, she could be a surprising girl sometimes, she thought to herself as she poured a cup of steaming dark brown liquid into her mug.

Truth be told, she had never written as quickly or as confidently as she had on this piece, this novel, as it was finally turning out to be. But then again, she had never felt like she did when she was in the presence of a certain cowboy, either. He was a good luck charm at the very least. And an excellent kisser. She shivered as she remembered what it felt like to have his arms encircle her. She smiled to herself and raised the mug of coffee to take a sip.

"Back to work," she told herself aloud as if there was someone there to hold her accountable. "You don't have time for daydreaming. Not yet, anyway."

It only took a couple more hours to finish the book. When she finally typed the words "the end", the sun had fully risen and was casting its delightful warm rays throughout her cabin. Claire stood up and exclaimed "Victory!" before doing a little jig, which ended with her dissolving into laughter at how absurd she must look. But nonetheless, the first draft of the book was done, it was some of her best work, and she knew exactly why.

The main house was silent in the morning glow as Claire peeked out her guest cabin window. Her eyes were immediately drawn to the rocking chairs, where Cole had kissed her, where he had lit such a fire in her. She knew that was why she had finished her book. Claire had taken all of that energy and emotion and let it burn slowly through her, all night long. She had let it breathe life into each word she put down on the page. And now it was done, and a day early at that! The publishing house was going to, hopefully, lose their collective minds with joy.

But that kiss... with her work completed, Claire couldn't, wouldn't stop her mind from dwelling on it. Her stomach began to twist.

Before she knew it, her coffee mug was empty. How long had she been standing there daydreaming, lost in thought? Well, she supposed it was entirely possible she had actually been dreaming for real. There was a good chance she had fallen asleep standing up. She yawned and stretched her limbs, holding the coffee cup with a couple of fingers.

The sun had completely taken over the sky now, banishing the night and its dark musings. The birds were singing their morning songs, prairie dogs were chirping at one another, and a slight breeze made the grass dance slowly and lazily. It was perfect.

Claire turned back toward her computer. She made sure her manuscript was backed up in several places; there was no way she was going to lose all of that work. As she double-checked her file for the hundredth time, Claire realized she was going to have to go into town to send it out. There was no way she would have enough cell signal to use her phone as a hotspot, and she really did want to get the manuscript out as soon as possible. It was time to relax, with the work being done. And if that relaxing happened to take place in a certain cowboy's arms… well, Claire wouldn't complain about that.

The coffee coursing through her veins convinced her that she didn't need a nap, just a shower. Within an hour Claire and her laptop were loaded up in the rental Smart-car and headed off to see Morning Star. The drive seemed to go quicker than it had before. Whether from her lack of sleep or her excitement, Claire didn't know or care.

The coffee shop was empty, as it had been during her previous visits. Claire sailed in with an air of excitement and accomplishment. She grinned stupidly at Morning Star as the kind woman made her yet another coffee. Claire didn't dare count how many that would make for her in the last twenty-four hours.

"You are kind of creeping me out with that smile there," Morning Star commented as a burst of steam lifted from the machine she was working on.

"Sorry," Claire said, even though she wasn't sorry at all. "I haven't really slept, and it might be catching up with me."

"Oh?" Morning Star glanced up from her work, eyebrows raised high. "And why is that?"

"It's nothing like that!" Claire almost felt the need to defend herself. "At least not yet."

Morning Star finished up the two lattes and headed toward their traditional table. She sat down as she placed the two mugs across from each other. Claire collapsed in a chair and hoisted her laptop case onto the table.

"I finished it," she said triumphantly as she unzipped the case, pulled out the laptop, and turned it on.

"The book? Wow! That's great!" Claire's friend congratulated her genuinely. "You got that done a lot quicker than you thought you were going to."

"Let's just say I had some good inspiration," Claire confessed. "There!" she said, closing the laptop with a giant smile on her face. "It's off to the publisher, and I am free! For the moment, anyway."

"That's really wonderful. I'm so happy for you." Morning Star smiled over her coffee mug. "The latte is definitely on the house today. When do I get to read it?" Her eyebrows raised in question.

"Soon!" Claire said triumphantly. She was starting to feel a little lightheaded. Maybe all the coffee was finally starting to get to her, but she felt too giddy to really care.

"What will you do now?" Morning Star asked. "You still have a couple of days left of your trip, don't you?"

Claire toyed with the handle of her mug and didn't meet her friend's eyes. "I plan on relaxing a little, see where the winds of fate lead me."

"I'll take that as writer-speak for having fun with a certain cowboy."

"What do you know about it?" Claire jerked her eyes up to meet Morning Star's. She was surprised to find an amused look on the woman's face. "I thought you said he was bad news."

"Oh, you can't believe everything you hear in this town," Morning Star said. "I should know."

"What do you know?" Claire couldn't resist asking. The kiss had been wonderful, but if there was other information to confirm the man's feelings, she needed to know.

"Well, if you were to ask me," Morning Star paused to take a sip of her coffee, drawing out her answer.

"Stop it!" Claire exclaimed, throwing both hands up in the air in mock frustration. "Tell me already!"

"If I didn't know better, I'd say he has a crush on you."

"Really?"

"Oh, yes. I've been around enough lovesick bull cows to know one when I see one."

Claire couldn't help the grin that spread across her face, or the butterflies that started going off in her stomach. She clasped her hands around her mug in an effort to keep them from shaking.

"Well," she tried to say calmly. "Cole is okay, for a cowboy."

"Mmmmhmmmm," came the hummed response.

"It's not too early in the year for a little summer fling, right?" Claire asked.

"A summer fling, eh? Is that what you're calling it?" Morning Star took another sip of coffee, letting her words sink in. "I suppose not. If that's what you two are looking for."

"The book will be published next year," Claire said, changing the subject and hoping her face wasn't a bright tomato red. "Things move slowly in the publishing world. But I bet I can get you an early reader copy."

"Whatever you say, dear," Morning Star said, leaning back in her chair. "Whatever you say."

They chatted over trivial things for the next half hour before Claire decided that she needed to go. She really did need to get a nap in before she fell asleep standing up. The sun was high in the sky when she pulled out of town. Plenty of time left in the day to take the horses out or help replenish the woodpile or find a reason to trip into Cole's arms. Just as soon as she got a cat nap.

"Oh yes," Claire told the rental car as she drove along the highway. "I am most certainly delusional." The lack of sleep was definitely getting to her, but she didn't care. She was on a real vacation now that her manuscript was turned in.

The cell phone, which was sitting on the passenger seat of the car, began to chirp and vibrate with an incoming call. Claire picked it up without hesitation or taking her eyes off the road. It would be Grace, her best friend and editor, calling to congratulate her on having completed the manuscript, and early at that!

"Keep the bubbly chilled!" Claire said excitedly by way of greeting. "I'm on vacation now!"

"Bubbly does sound very, very nice," a smooth, male voice cooed through the phone.

Claire's hand was instantly clammy, and she nearly dropped the phone. "Chad?" It was an effort not to call him "Stupid Chad."

"Yes, darling. It's me." Still so confident, so self-assured.

"I, ah, what," Claire tried to stall, her tired, fuzzy mind trying to find words to say. She was not winning. She focused on the road as if somehow driving would save her.

"I was in Grace's office when your email came through," Chad didn't even notice that she was struggling to talk to him. He just plowed on ahead, as ever. "I'm so glad your manuscript is finished. I'd be happy to read over it for you..." he trailed off suggestively.

Of course, he would be happy to read over it. He always had loved pointing out her mistakes and shortcomings. "No. That's quite all right. Grace is quite capable of handling the editing." Claire didn't know how she was managing to stay so calm. Maybe it was the way his voice still stirred the embers in her belly.

"Sure, sure. But you know my door is always open for you," Chad readily agreed. "I've been thinking a lot about you. About us..."

Claire didn't respond. She could barely keep the phone to her ear, her hand was shaking so hard.

"I'm sorry, for what happened between us." Chad's words caused Claire to slam on the breaks as she turned off the highway onto the road leading to the ranch.

Those words, how she had longed to hear them for months and months and months. He was sorry. Well, part of her mind had something to say about that. The man hadn't actually said he was sorry for what he had done, just that he was sorry for how it had ended. But was there really that much of a difference between the two? Claire's tired mind warred with itself, and she realized she hadn't said anything into the phone.

"Yeah," she finally made her tongue choke out. "Me too."

"I want you back." Those words made her heart stop.

"Wh...what? What did you say?"

"I want you back, Claire. I need you back," Chad said, with all the confidence in the world. "I need our late-night editing sessions back."

The way he said it, how his voice got low and sexy, Claire knew exactly what "editing sessions" he was referring too. And in that instant, she wanted them back too.

"I... ah..." She still couldn't form words, but her body was responding to his words, and her mind played images of Chad's arms encircling her deep in the night.

"Think about it," Chad cooed. "I know you want me back. I know you remember how good we were together. We can be even better together now that your manuscript is done. I'll help you make it even better."

"I... how?" Claire couldn't form the right words. Her emotions and feelings were all over the place. A bird flew right in front of her, so she stopped the rental car and watched it until it disappeared into the sun. She was unable to form thoughts that made any kind of sense.

"Call me when you decide," Chad commanded. "I'm sure it won't be long before I hear from you." And with that, he was gone.

Claire lowered the phone from her ear and stared dumbly at the screen. Chad had ended the call without so much as a coherent word from her. But he had said he wanted her again, hadn't he? And he had apologized! Claire had never thought she would see the day.

She gently lowered her foot to the gas pedal and the little rental car surged forward, Claire's thoughts following suit. Sure, she told herself, she could have a summer fling with a cowboy. But Chad, he was someone who was already integrated into her life. He made sense. He was who she should be with. He could be constant and steadfast. Cole would be a few days of fun, and that's it.

Her mind was spinning out of control. Chad had hurt her so badly, but if he was genuinely apologetic… they could maybe go back to the way things had been before it had turned ugly. All of this kept going through her head, over and over, as she turned onto the drive of Paradise Valley Ranch.

Next to the road, Claire saw Cole. He was putting up a large for-sale sign. Her heart threatened to constrict and stop beating altogether.

21. The For-Sale Sign

Every shovel full of dirt he dug up felt like a small betrayal to his ancestry. Of course, Cole knew that every one of his family members who had worked this land, they would never have blamed him for what he had to do. He knew this was best. He knew he was doing the right thing. But placing the for-sale sign into the land felt like stabbing himself in the heart.

Patrick Cole watched from the corner of his eye as the tiny Smart-car slowly pulled up the drive and parked next to his work truck. Part of him wanted to be alone with his misery, but part of him also desperately needed someone to tell him it was all going to be okay. Buck wasn't any help at all. The dog was lying next to the truck, not even remotely interested in chasing prairie dogs, as if he too felt the severity of the situation.

Claire slowly got out of her car, as if she couldn't decide if she was intruding or not. Cole packed the dirt around the sign one more time and then picked up his tools and headed for his truck. He opened the tailgate and threw the shovel and post hole digger into the bed of the truck. They landed with a devastating clatter that matched his mood.

"Hi," his guest said softly as she walked up to him. Or was she more than a guest now, after their shared, passionate kiss? Cole didn't know. Despite Chuck's advice, he didn't know that he was in the right kind of mindset to do anything about his feelings toward the beautiful woman. He nodded to her in greeting, not entirely trusting his voice.

"You're going to sell." She didn't say it like a question, but Cole felt the need to answer anyway.

"Yes," his voice cracked, and he leaned against the tailgate, focusing on his mud-covered boots.

"Oh, Cole," her voice was soft and enveloped him in a warm, comforting way. "I am so, so sorry."

He only nodded, not able to look up from his boots. The tourist came to stand next to him and placed a small hand on his arm.

"I know how much this land means to you."

Cole brought his head up and looked her in the eyes. He could see such compassion there, he wanted to break down and snuggle himself into her arms, where he knew he would find some sort of peace. But he held himself steady; he didn't know if that's where either of them wanted this to go.

"Yeah," was all he managed to choke out. He moved to sit on the tailgate. Claire joined him. While he only had to shift himself, she had to hop a little bit to get herself up onto the tailgate. In the back of his mind, Cole thought it was adorable. Perhaps, just maybe, he could unburden himself, just a little, to his tourist.

"I can't believe I am doing this," he said quietly, looking out across the land rather than at the beautiful woman at his side. "I've worked so hard, for so long. And not a lick of it mattered in the end. I've failed." His voice cracked on the last two words. Cole, for the first time since he didn't know how long, felt tears sting his eyes.

Claire sat silently next to him, listening, waiting, not pushing him, but patiently sitting with him. Cole swallowed hard several times in an effort to rein his emotions in. When he finally did look up, he gazed into Claire's beautiful face and saw her own tears glistening in her eyes. Cole couldn't move or say anything. He could only stare into those eyes that held him captive.

"I know," Claire said softly, her eyes not moving from his. "I know this is breaking your heart. I only wish there was something I could do to help."

Her words sunk deep into his soul, like a deep healing salve. It broke something loose in him, and he couldn't hold back the tears. Cole looked away from Claire's face to gaze out across the land his grandfather had worked for decades. The land he had worked himself to the bone to preserve.

"I've failed," he whispered as the tears dripped off of his unshaven chin.

Claire didn't say anything to his declaration, but she scooted closer to him on the tailgate and wrapped one arm around his lower back. Cole responded by letting his arm wrap around her in return. She leaned into him, and he let her. Her body felt good against his, tucked into him like that. Like an anchor that could help him stay steady in the face of the coming storm.

They sat there on the tailgate of the truck for who knew how long. The sun inched across the sky as dark clouds began to roll in. The weather suited Cole's mood just fine. Claire leaned her head against his shoulder, and he felt that if he could just hold onto this moment, everything would be fine.

But as all good things do, the moment came to an end. The

clouds rolled across the sun, and the wind picked up. A storm was definitely on the horizon. Both literally and figuratively, Cole thought.

He squeezed Claire's shoulder and said, "I think we should head back." He nodded toward the sky.

Claire nodded in agreement but seemed reluctant to move.

"Come on, honey," Cole said gently while untangling her from his own body. "We can go make dinner and relax in front of the fire. When the storm clouds look this dark, it means we are in for a bad one. We don't want to get caught out here in it."

They hopped down from the tailgate and silently moved to their respective vehicles. Cole opened his truck door and whistled, sharp and loud. Buck came bounding up and leaped into the truck. As Cole followed the dog, he turned toward Claire's rental, where she was sliding into the driver's seat, and tipped his hat. Her face lit up into a smile, and she tipped an imaginary hat back.

As both cars lumbered down the long drive to the main house, Cole found himself trying to focus on the future, rather than on his failure and the sale of his family land. Perhaps the day wasn't a total loss after all.

* * *

Claire followed behind Cole's truck in her little rental car. She was amazed that just a few days ago, she had been in a very similar situation, but a muddy mess and furious with who she had thought was the rudest cowboy to ever walk the earth. It seemed like a lifetime ago. A lifetime ago, when she had shown up broken and beaten down by the world.

Rolling down the window, she breathed in deeply. The air

smelled faintly of rain and wind and fog. This land had changed her. It had taken hold of her shattered heart and melded it back together. Not to mention a certain dimpled man who had helped her find the courage to step outside of herself, step out of the box she had allowed herself to be put in for so many years.

She was more than just a bestselling author. Though Lord knew she was grateful for that. But she was also a woman who had learned to stack firewood, ride a horse, study fence line, cook tacos, and dance under the glittering light of a thousand stars.

Chad's phone call had stunned her. It was what she had wanted for so long. As Claire breathed in the mountain air again, she knew Stupid Chad wasn't what she wanted any longer.

She would not allow herself to be turned into a big-time editor's pet, which was all Chad had ever really wanted, in the end. It was why he took her out to all the big parties and insisted she stay on his arm the entire evening. It was why the man had always sent her flowers through her publishing house so that everyone might see them. It was why he wanted to make a tour of all the bookstores in the upper state of New York. She had never been more than a plaything to the man.

The realization didn't stun her in a traditional way, but it did take her breath away. Her foot eased off the gas pedal, just for a moment. As if he sensed her falling behind, Buck's head poked up over the seat of the truck and looked out the back window. He was grinning, as always.

"Ridiculous dog," Claire said aloud, even though she knew perfectly well the dog couldn't hear her. Although he did cock his head to the side at her words. Claire couldn't help but laugh at the timing.

21. The For-Sale Sign

Now that her decision was made concerning Stupid Chad, her thoughts were solely focused on her current predicament. Patrick Cole, mountain cowboy and a man of conviction. What was she going to do about him?

It felt like she had seen his heart cut open and laid out before her. She hated that he was going to have to sell his land. Hated that this ranch that she had fallen in love with was about to be turned over to some billionaire who would use it as an occasional mountain retreat to be shown off to friends. It wasn't right. Not after all the sweat and blood Cole had sewn into the very land itself. But she was powerless to change that. It was beyond her control. If it were her novel, she would have written all the cowboy's dreams coming true. For now, though, she would provide him what little comfort she could. Well, they would comfort each other, really. What they could have was only a few days of a summer fling before the western fairy tale ran out of time.

The thought both saddened and excited Claire. It was an odd mixture of emotions to experience, and she contributed most of the confusion to her lack of sleep. In fact, she was sure it would make her start seeing things at any moment.

The truck pulled up in front of the main house, and Claire pulled her rental car right up beside it. Buck grinned at her from the passenger seat, like he knew some sort of summer fling shenanigans were about to happen. Claire grinned back. She caught a glance of Cole's amused smile as she climbed out of her car.

"That dog might try to sneak in your suitcase when you leave," he said, leaning against the bed of the truck, his arms crossed over the side. "I think he might like you better than me." The cowboy winked at her, setting her heart into a gallop.

"That's just because he doesn't remember who feeds him," Claire teased as the dog leaped out of the truck and trotted over to her as she walked around the tailgate. When she neared Cole, she crouched down to bestow some love on the poor neglected dog.

"Maybe not," Cole said and chuckled. "But he does remember who has been throwing that tennis ball for him every morning." As Claire stood up, he reached and felt her bicep. "I do declare," he said in an exaggerated accent, "your arm does seem to be much stronger than when you first arrived."

He winked again, stealing Claire's breath away, and began to pull her into a hug. As she came into his arms, he leaned back against the truck. In Claire's sleep-deprived mind, she bet they looked like a romance novel book cover. Well, except that she was a mess in yesterday's clothes and he still had his shirt on. She inhaled deeply, relaxing into Cole's arms. But a novel cover, nonetheless.

Then her mind kicked in. She was a mess! A true mess. She couldn't start a summer love affair with her hair askew and smelling like she'd slept in her clothes. She broke their embrace and stepped away from Cole. She watched him raise his eyebrows in question.

"I… uh…" Claire scrambled for words that wouldn't sound completely foolish. "I should freshen up. Before dinner, I mean." She gestured down at her wrinkled clothes and started to pull at her tangled hair.

"If you say so," Cole drawled, but reached out for her hand. He pulled her close and wrapped his arms around her. It felt like he had lit a fire within Claire and it threatened to consume her completely. "I'll just be in the kitchen."

He didn't wait for her to respond before he lowered his head and found her lips with his. Claire closed her eyes, her arms sliding around the cowboy's lower back. In her mind she narrated, it was the kiss to end all kisses. Somewhere deep inside herself, Claire wanted to roll her eyes at that, but she couldn't. She was too happy to do anything but half smile as she returned the kiss.

Buck had apparently thought the kiss had gone on quite long enough because he started to yip and nip at Cole's boots. They broke off the kiss but continued to stare into each other's eyes, both panting just the slightest bit. Cole waved the dog off with his hand, careful not to break eye contact.

Claire stepped back, her legs feeling a little bit wobbly and her head felt light. "I'll be right back," she managed.

"I'll be here," Cole said with a seductive edge on his voice. "I'm not going anywhere. Not yet, anyway. Hurry, that storm is rolling in."

It took all the willpower Claire had to turn away from him and head toward her cabin. She self-consciously pulled at her t-shirt. She really did need to freshen up. But she promised herself she would be quick about it. Very quick.

22. The Girlfriend

Claire took the fastest shower of her life, barely making sure she had properly rinsed the soap and shampoo off before she hopped out and began to towel off. Her excitement was palpable. The burn Cole had lit in her with his kiss had not died down; if anything, it had grown. Claire couldn't, no, wouldn't stop thinking about it.

She quickly changed into a new, clean t-shirt, popped on her new earrings, pulled on her favorite pair of jeans, which made her ass look amazing, and stood in front of the mirror trying to decide what to do about her out-of-control mane. In the end, she pulled it over to one side and worked it into a single braid, hoping it wouldn't be staying put for long anyway. She studied herself in the mirror, and despite the bags under her eyes, she thought she looked acceptable. Even if she hadn't, that burn inside of her wasn't going to let her stay in her cabin much longer. It yearned to be fanned and stoked by a certain cowboy. The dark bags under her eyes could go hang themselves.

Claire jerked back to reality and realized she had been

standing in front of the mirror, daydreaming, for who knew how long. "For heaven's sake," she scolded herself. "You'd think I'd never kissed a man before."

After one more once-over in the mirror, and a last-minute adjustment to her shirt, Claire deemed herself ready enough. The sky had darkened. As she glanced out the backdoor of the cabin, she thought it was in part because it was getting later and in part because of the dark clouds that were rolling in quickly across the fields. A storm might invoke a cozy night of snuggling by the fire. Claire was pretty sure she could handle that. That and more. She felt a blush rise to her cheeks, much to her chagrin.

"Get a grip," she told herself as she walked toward the cabin door.

It was then that she heard tires on the driveway. It had better not be that old man, here to spoil my fun again, Claire mused to herself, only half joking. But rather than come barreling out the door of her cabin in some twisted effort to save her romantic evening, she decided to take a glance out of the window first. Claire shook her head as if barreling out the front door was going to save anything. She really needed to get a grip or a take nice long nap... maybe a nap in Cole's arms.

The vehicle speeding up the drive, kicking up a storm of dust behind it, was not the truck that the old man had been driving. No, this was a little two-door car – red, sporty, and fast. The windows were tinted. Claire squinted as if she was going to be able to see who was behind the wheel. She sighed as the little car came to an abrupt stop behind Cole's truck. The little sports car laid on its horn, surprising everyone from Claire to the quail that suddenly took flight near the house.

Cole stepped out of the house, a deep scowl on his face. Until he saw the car, that is. Once he saw it, his face broke out into a huge grin. Claire could visibly see his body relax, and then he was trotting down the steps, happy as a clam.

The red sports-car driver-side door swung open, and it was like Claire was watching it in slow motion. A beautiful, tall woman got out of the car, her rich, golden-brown hair catching glints of what little sun hadn't been entirely hidden by the dark clouds. The woman was long and lean, dressed in shorts and a tank top. She was perfect, by Claire's summation.

And Cole must have thought so too. Because as the two met, somewhere between the vehicles and the house, the cowboy picked up the perfect woman and swung her in a wide circle, going around and around. When he finally put the woman back on solid ground, she slugged his arm, but Claire could see that the woman was laughing with abandon. Cole slung his arm around the woman and led her up the front stair and into the house, out of site.

As the door closed behind them, Claire felt like she had been punched in the gut. Or maybe it felt like she had suddenly contracted a violent strand of the flu. The lack of sleep made it hard to tell. It also made it hard to sort through her raging emotions. They were a tsunami that Claire could not escape.

She finally stopped staring after the couple, and at the door they had disappeared behind. Her hand fell to her side, letting the curtain fall back over the window she had been spying through. Claire took several steps back and sat down heavily on her unmade bed. Were her hands shaking? Surely not. She buried them under her thighs as she started to chew on her lower lip, a nervous habit.

Who was the woman in the red car? Why was Cole so glad to see her? Why had he now, seemingly, forgotten all about her? The questions whirled faster and faster in Claire's mind, threatening to make her sick.

Cole would come and explain, Claire told herself. Any moment now, there would be a knock on her cabin door, and he would be standing there, explaining that the woman was some long-lost aunt he hadn't seen in years. She had come to inform him that she had written him into her will. Claire shook her head. She was really going off the rails. That woman, all tall and beautiful, was clearly not a long-lost aunt.

All of the rumors Morning Star had mentioned began to sink their ugly claws into Claire's tired mind. Maybe the woman was one of Cole's fabled girlfriends. Come to think of it, Claire had written a scene, just like the one she had just witnessed, in one of her novels. The couple had been destined to be together, and they lived happily ever after.

That must be it. Cole and the red sports car woman were lovers, destined to be together. Perhaps, she was this Julie that Cole had mentioned several times. The very woman who decorated this very guest cabin.

Claire felt all of her dreams and hopes of a summer romance shatter into a thousand tiny pieces. She should have known better. She should have known that it wasn't going to work out. A tear or two leaked out of the corners of Claire's eyes. Her heart told her that it couldn't be true, but her head knew that it was. It was going to be like losing Chad all over again.

She would end up losing herself in some sort of deep loathing, waiting for a man to take her back. Her work would suffer, and she would suffer, again.

Claire suddenly found herself on her feet. Not again. She would not let herself fall into that trap. She had learned something about herself in her time writing this last project in Montana. She was stronger than she had thought. She had learned how to stack firewood after all. And how to ride a horse!

A horse, she mused. That was it! She knew how to saddle, sort of, and ride a horse. Before she gave herself a second to think it through, she was headed out the door of the guest cabin and toward the corral. She didn't bother to grab her phone, it's not like she had cell signal anyway. She didn't bother to close the door of the cabin either. She was on a mission, to prove something to herself... and maybe that blasted cowboy too.

Scout was the only horse in the corral. He was prancing in a circle, showing off for Claire. It brought a quick smile to her face. Though she had only ridden the gentle Lady in her time at Paradise Valley Ranch, she felt sure that she was experienced enough now to take on a bigger challenge. Hadn't she already been thrown once before? It was clear to her that she should saddle the horse up and take him out for a ride. Lady wasn't in sight, after all. Just the prancing, proud Scout, the cowboy's horse.

Claire found the tack in the barn and had Scout saddled in no time. She rushed through the process, not wanting to remember how she learned, how close Cole had been to her when he was teaching her, how even then she had wanted his arms around her.

She had a difficult time trying to mount the horse. Scout kept skittering to the side, ready to take off and ride with the wind that was pushing the prairie grass in all sorts of direction. Scout was as ready for an adventure as Claire was. Good, she thought, as she finally got herself up on the horse's back.

The horse sidestepped as her full weight settled on him, but then stood patiently, waiting for her command. Claire sucked in a deep breath, threw one last look at the ranch house, hoping Cole would appear and have some sort of explanation. When he didn't, she leaned down and stroked Scout's long neck.

"What do you say?" she whispered to the horse, who whinnied in reply.

Claire sat up straight in the saddle and nudged her knees into the horse's sides. They took off like a shot out of the ranch yard, headed straight for the range where she had helped Cole check the fence line, straight toward those unforgivable, beautiful mountains.

23. The Tourist

A thunderclap rolled across the prairie, causing Cole to jerk his head up from his mug of coffee and look out the kitchen door. He had known when he saw the clouds starting to roll in earlier that it was going to be a bad storm. After spending his entire life on this land, he could read it better than anyone. Even his granddaddy had told him so, at one point or another.

He expected to see the sky darkened and angry when he looked up. But instead, he saw a flash of white and long hair flying by. "What the devil?" he said aloud, causing Julie to look up from her own cup of coffee.

"What?" she asked, her face the picture of innocence.

"Damn, fool tourist," Cole grumbled as he grabbed his hat off the hook by the door. "What the hell does she think she's doing, riding out just as a storm is stirring up?"

"What?" Julie said again, forehead furrowed and eyebrows lifted. "What are you talking about?"

Cole shook his head, put on his hat, and growled, "I'll be back." He was out the door without a backward glance.

23. *The Tourist*

It didn't take him long to cross the ranch yard and realize that Claire had taken Scout. "Damn it all to hell," he cursed as he entered the barn. He grabbed a bridle from a peg and headed out to the side pasture, where he had let Lady out to graze earlier in the day.

The mare was waiting for him, and he closed the distance between him and the side pasture with long, angry strides. Lady tossed her head in greeting, probably hoping for some treat, an apple or a carrot. Cole reached out and rubbed her nose.

"Not today, dear," he said and then slide the bridle onto her head. "The tourist needs rescuing again." The edge and grit in his voice surprised him, but then again, this wasn't the first time that fool woman had needed rescuing. But this time she had put herself in a much more dangerous predicament.

Having secured the bridle, Cole rubbed the mare's nose one last time and then swung up onto her bareback. She shuffled sideways, unaccustomed to being ridden without a saddle, but she settled quick enough, and they set off at a quick trot out of the ranch yard. Cole caught a glance of Julie standing on the porch of the house, her eyes following him as he headed out in the direction he had seen Claire go.

A million different things were running through his head as he and Lady hit the open prairie of his land. Why in the hell would Claire take off like that? And just as a storm was starting to ramp up! How foolish could she be? And taking Scout? He'd told her the horse was a little skittish. That was why he put her on good, old, gentle Lady in the first place.

A thunderclap burst so hard across the prairie that Cole thought it might split that land open in front of him and swallow him whole. Then the raindrops started. Slow and light at first, like a kind of spring shower. But as he pressed closer to the mountains, the rain became heavier, violent even. They pelted down like they were trying to take vengeance against the whole world.

The weather could be like that, Cole knew. It could be so peaceful and then ten minutes later it could be trying to kill you. He knew that all right, but Claire didn't. Hell, she barely knew how to saddle a horse. He was half impressed the tourist had gotten Scout to corporate with her, but Cole quickly let that feeling dissolve into anger. How dare she just take off like this?

He was soaked through and could no longer follow Scout's tracks; they were washed away by the enormous raindrops that continued to beat down against the land. Lady did not want to be out in this weather, but she was gamely trotting along as if she knew there was an urgent reason they were out in the bad weather in the first place.

Everything was dark. Though the sun had yet to dip below the mountain line, the storm clouds blocked out any of its bright rays. It might as well have been the darkest night without any star or moonlight. Flashes of lightning in the distance lit the sky every few minutes, but they were too far off to make any real difference. Without any light or tracks to follow, Cole was basically looking for a needle in a haystack, and he knew it. He sent a quick prayer out to the universe. He was going to need all the help he could get.

As the words left his lips in a silent prayer, a spike of lightning shot across the sky right above them. It scared the hell out of both horse and rider. Cole's legs involuntarily tightened around the mare, and she half reared, trying to shake him off. He tried to sooth the horse and apologize, but another thunderclap cut him off.

23. *The Tourist*

Cole shot a glance up at the sky. This storm was going to be worse than he expected. He needed to find Claire, and he needed to find her now.

As if in response to his thought, another spike of lightning flashed across the sky, right above them. As the light reverberated across the prairie land and into the mountains Cole caught a glance of a horse, running wild in the direction of the ranch house. He squinted, waiting for another flash to light the sky. He didn't have to wait long. There was the horse, and yes, it was definitely Scout bolting for home.

But there wasn't a rider on the horse. The reins drooped, and the saddle was empty. Fear struck deep in Cole's heart. That fool tourist better not have gotten herself killed, he thought and pushed Lady into a gallop. He headed in the direction Scout had been running from.

Cole's eyes scanned open prairie with each flash of lightning, half hoping he wouldn't spot Claire, half hoping he would. She had to be safe. She just had to be. He would allow nothing less on his land. Period.

They slowed up, just a little bit, as they approached the back fence-line near the mountains and forest. It half occurred to Cole that he was riding very near to where Lady had thrown Claire. That seemed a lifetime ago. Damn it. His life before Claire seemed a lifetime ago. That wasn't something he wanted to think about right now.

Another flash of lightning and Cole thought he saw a figure, limping along the fence-line. His heart lurched, and he felt like he had to swallow it back down. Let her be all right; he sent another prayer out into the universe. Just let her be okay.

He leaned over the horse and urged her into a full gallop, heading straight for the ghostly outlined figure. It felt like an eternity to cross the distance between them. Cole could finally see that it was Claire, as if anyone else would be out in this storm. Her hair was dripping into her face. Her limp was far worse than it had seemed when he had first spotted her. It didn't appear that she had seen him yet. She was fumbling along the fence line, trying to do God knew what.

Cole slid from Lady's back a few feet from Claire. He held the reins tight as Lady sidestepped nervously and he reached for Claire's arm. She screamed, and he could barely hear it over the wind and thunder. But as soon as she saw it was him, relief flooded her eyes, and Cole was sure there were tears mixed with the rain flowing down her face.

She fell into his arms awkwardly and clung to him. She was unharmed, for the most part. And it didn't hurt that she was apparently glad to see him. Cole felt himself sigh in relief as he wrapped his arms around her, trying not to be too obvious as he prodded at her back to make sure there were no broken bones. Thankfully, as far as he could tell, there weren't.

He brought his mouth down close to her ear and fought to be heard over the thunder that now seemed unceasing. "Are you okay?"

Claire only nodded her head against his chest and tightened her arms around him. It made his heart beat just a little faster. But this wasn't any kind of time to be thinking about romantic ideas. They had to get to safety. Now.

As if the universe sensed their predicament, the storm suddenly began to move away. Dark clouds headed east, leaving behind a dark-gray mess that leaked heavy raindrops. The worst of the storm had passed, almost as quickly as it had rolled in. God bless Montana's fickle weather, Cole thought with no small amount of relief.

Lady was skittering, pulling at the reins, but still able to carry them back to the ranch house. Cole would build a fire and hold Claire until she felt safe and warm again. They might actually get out of this unscathed. He pulled down a deep breath and prepared to help Claire onto the horse.

A mountain lion screamed. Cole cursed as he fought to hold onto the horse's reins as she jerked and pulled. It forced Claire to stumble back, to keep out of the horse's way. The rain was pounding down in hard, thick drops again.

Another scream cut through the air. This time the mare reared and Cole lost his grip on the slick reins entirely. Lady took off like a shot, headed straight back toward the ranch and the comfort of a warm stall.

Cole watched her go in disbelief. This was just not his day, he thought. What the hell were they going to do now?

Claire had been stunned out of her tears as the horse fled. She now stood staring toward the rolling hills it had disappeared over. Finally, she turned her eyes toward him. Cole read sheer terror there. The tourist had probably never even dreamed of a situation even remotely close to this, writer or no. She just stood there, dripping, and trying to hold back more tears.

Cole started to act without thinking his plan all the way through. He took Claire's hand and pulled her toward the fence line. He held the barbed wire as far apart as he could to let her crawl through and then followed behind her. Cole led them toward the forest. Claire looked confused, but limped behind him, even as she started to shiver.

Out here in a t-shirt and soaking wet, Cole thought. At least he'd had the sense to grab a jacket.

He walked them right up to the forest line and then into the trees, with her hand clinging to his like a lifeline. Cole didn't stop until he found exactly what he was looking for. Then he bent down and crawled under a tree, pulling the tourist with him.

The ground was dry, and the pine tree branches seemed to close in around them, lending the couple it's protection. Cole sat against the tree trunk and shrugged out of his jacket. He pulled Claire close to him and helped her into the coat. She leaned against him, still trying to keep the tears at bay. Cole held her close and rubbed up and down her back and arms, trying to get some warmth back into her.

"You had to rescue me," Claire said through chattering teeth. "Again, damn you."

"Well you had to go get yourself into another fool situation which you needed rescuing from," Cole said against her wet hair. "Next time, I'll remember to ignore you."

"You do that." Her shivering had calmed more quickly than he could have hoped. And he took the banter as a good sign. But he was worried about her ankle and the fast-approaching night.

"You aren't supposed to be around trees in a thunderstorm," she piped up, but her voice sounded drowsy.

"Well, the worst of the storm has passed. And it's drier under here," Cole explained, slowing his rapid rubbing on her arms. "We might have to stay here for the night. I don't know how bad your ankle is, but I don't want to risk injuring it further by bumbling around in the dark."

He hugged her close and realized she had already fallen asleep. Cole closed his eyes and felt her chest rise and fall with each breath. He hunkered down a little further into the tree shelter and settled in for the night. Truth be told, there were worse ways to spend an evening than under a tree with a beautiful woman in your arms. Even if she were a fool of a tourist that had almost gotten herself killed.

24. The Sister

The sun was bright and as beautiful as ever when Claire dragged herself out from underneath the pine tree the next morning. Her body was stiff and sore, and her ankle was screaming at her, but at least the sun was shining and Montana was breathtaking, as it always was. Be that as it may, she never wanted to see another dark cloud as long as she lived.

Claire groaned and stretched out her limbs as she watched Cole crawl out from underneath the same tree. The man didn't look like he had gotten more than a wink or two of sleep. Whereas she had slept the entire night through and part of the morning, having only woken a few minutes before. She blinked rapidly, trying to the clear the sleep from her eyes and the stupid idea of a summer fling from her head.

"Did you sleep at all?" she asked, trying to suppress a yawn and failing.

"A little," the cowboy replied. He didn't look at her. He was concentrating on the landscape.

Claire couldn't help but look that way too. She only saw the paradise she knew this land to be. No sign of the nightmarish storm that had tried to kill her the day before. Claire tried to resist the shudder that ran through her at the thought. But then a different kind of thought took hold in her mind. A thought that had caused her to saddle a horse and ride off into the middle of a storm. A thought that ruined any amount of joy she had found since arriving on Paradise Valley Ranch.

Cole took a step toward her and made a move to put his arm around her. Claire jerked herself away before he had the chance, stumbling as pain shot up her ankle. She must have done some real damage to it the day before. Awesome. Just what she needed.

Claire glanced up and watched as a stunned express spread over the cowboy's face, then as his eyes narrowed. Yes, she thought, we are both spoiling for a fight right now. Let's do it.

Claire shrugged out of his jacket, which she had worn all through the night, and shivered as the cool air breathed against her bare arms, but she was determined. She held the jacket out to Cole, who made no move to take it. The tension between them was so thick it was almost suffocating. Finally, Claire let the jacket fall from the finger she had been balancing it on. Neither took their eyes from each other as it piled on the ground in a small heap.

When Claire couldn't take the juvenile staring contest any longer, she broke the silence between them. "You really are something else, Patrick Cole, cowboy extraordinaire."

Cole blinked once, slowly. Then he exploded. "I am something else? Me!?"

Claire took an involuntary step backward at his outburst, but it redoubled her own anger. She wasn't going to back down, not when she had been so wronged. She straightened her spine and stood to her full height. She glared at him, hoping her eyes said "you don't scare me, little cowboy."

"I am not the fool that rode off into that storm!" Cole continued, his voice rising with each word until he was full on shouting. "I'm not the tourist who thought I was above Nature herself!" He flung his arms out as if Nature herself would show up and back his argument, right then and there.

"No one died!" Claire shot back, ignoring the pain in her ankle and the wave of terror, left over from the night before, that threatened to take over her emotions. "Besides, I'm not the one that lied."

She stated those last few words as if they made her point entirely. Case closed.

"Lied?" the word hissed out of Cole's clenched teeth. "Lied? This is ridiculous. Who the hell lied to you?"

Claire's mouth dropped open, but she snapped it shut and balled her fists at her sides. This was going to get ugly. She opened her mouth to spew an argument at her cowboy host, but he cut her off by throwing his arms up into the air.

"And that would not be a good a reason to try and get yourself killed!"

"No one died!" Claire shouted back as if that kind of an argument made any sort of sense. It really didn't, and she knew it, but she was too far gone to think of anything better.

They stood in the middle of the prairie, ignoring the sun, ignoring the beauty around them, steam practically coming out of their ears. It might as well have been a good old-fashioned wild-wild-west standoff. Neither party blinked. They barely breathed.

"You lied to me." Claire hated that her voice was cracking. "You lied to me, and I didn't know what else to do." Her hair hung like a curtain over her face as Claire found the sudden need to study a blade of grass at her feet.

Cole took a step toward her, she could feel it, and his boot entered her field of vision as she continued to study the ground. She could feel the tears beginning to well up in her eyes. From lack of sleep, disappointment, her ankle, Cole's proximity to her. Did it even matter anymore?

The cowboy's voice was soft and gentle as he said, "Claire, what are you talking about?"

It triggered a full flood of tears that Claire couldn't hold back. She just wanted everything to go back to the way it had been yesterday before the red sports car had driven down the lane. When her hopes and dreams had been alive and well, rather than broken into a million pieces with no hope of ever being put back together again. Salty tears dripped off her nose, and she couldn't help but sniff, but she refused to look up. Refused to give the cowboy the satisfaction.

"Claire," his voice was soft again, just like it had been every time he had held her in his arms. It snapped something in Claire, and she jerked her head up, taking several limping steps back.

"All those rumors about you were right!" She flung the words at him as hard as she could. "You strung me along the whole time I was here, from the very beginning. Made a fool out of me!"

The cowboy's eyes were clouded like he didn't know what she was talking about. But Claire wasn't going to fall for that. She was no fool.

"Is she your girlfriend? Or just someone you sleep with? How many more are there? Why did you feel the need to mess with me at all? Clearly, I am not on your level."

Cole's body had tensed during her questions, and then some

sort of understanding dawned on him. Claire could practically see the wheels turning in his head. But she wasn't done.

"I had thought," her voice caught in her throat, "I had thought you were better than all the rest." When he didn't say anything, she continued. "I guess the cowboy hat and boots and the horseback riding and dancing under the stars… I guess you had me fooled good."

She felt a fresh wave of tears flow down her cheeks and did nothing to stop them. Let the dumb cowboy see the damage he had done. Maybe he would think twice when the next unsuspecting girl came along. Claire blinked, trying to clear her vision enough to glare daggers into the man's heart.

He made to move toward her, but she stiffened and held out a hand in warning. She accidentally placed too much pressure on the ankle and winced, but refused to give him the satisfaction of helping her.

"I don't have a girlfriend," he said, looking directly into her eyes. She barked out a short, hysterical laugh. That was rich.

"I don't," he confirmed. Claire couldn't help but roll her eyes.

"The woman, the one from last night," Cole didn't take his eyes from hers, didn't so much as blink. "That's my sister."

Claire blinked, once, slowly. His sister? How naive did this man think she was? She wasn't born yesterday. "Your sister," the words seethed. "You've never mentioned a sister."

"She…" Cole started, and then finally broke her gaze, as if he was searching for the right words. "She has been away for a while. And even before that, she wasn't around much." He sheepishly looked back up at her. "It didn't seem worth mentioning."

"Your sister," Claire couldn't help but repeat the words. She couldn't tell if they were sinking in or not, or if she even dared to believe him.

"I promise you, Claire," Cole took a step toward her, and this time she didn't pull away as he reached for her arm. "There is no other woman."

Claire finally loosened her grip on the anger and hurt. It began to bleed out of her, sliding out of her fingertips and dripping into the Montana soil. Her body shuddered with relief.

Without the anger to focus her, she realized how warm the sun felt against her bare skin, how blue the sky was, the wildflowers beginning to poke up in the spring weather, the weight and heat of the cowboy's hand on her arm. She closed her eyes and breathed in a deep breath through her nose, her shoulders slumping forward in relief.

"You promise?" Her voice sounded like a little girl's, even to her. But she thought it was understandable after what she had gone through in the last forty-eight hours. Claire opened her eyes slowly, looking into Cole's face, searching for the answer.

Cole nodded, taking a step closer and putting his free arm on hers, pulling her toward him. Claire almost melted into him, right then and there.

"Say it," she half demanded. She needed to hear those words, needed to listen to the truth in them.

"I promise," he breathed and looked deep into her eyes.

She believed him. Claire pressed into him then and let the tears flow. How she had any tears left after the last twenty-four hours, she had no idea. But this time, those tears were from relief and sheer joy.

"I can't stop thinking about you, even though you are a tourist. Even though you get stuck in mud puddles and ride off into storms. I can't get you out of my head," he said into her hair. "I think you've put some sort of spell on me."

She could feel the smile in his body language and let his words wash over her. She sighed and nestled her head into his chest even further. Her heart was happy, overjoyed. She couldn't even begin to find the words to express it. But she pulled back from him, just enough to look up into his eyes.

Claire pulled herself up on her tiptoes and kissed him. She looked like a wreck, they were standing between a forest and a field, and her ankle was throbbing, but she didn't care about any of that. It all faded away as his lips softly brushed hers and then pressed in a little harder. Cole's arms tightened, holding her close. Her arms slipped up around his neck and pulled him even closer to her. Their bodies melded into one another. It felt like home.

Claire didn't know how long they stood there like that, but they were both breathless as they pulled away from each other in tandem. Their arms continued to be wrapped around each other's bodies like they belonged there, like they belonged together. The cowboy and the tourist stood there grinning like fools, panting for the breath they had given to each other. Yes, it really did feel like home.

Claire jumped back from Cole's arms suddenly, sending a shooting pain up through her ankle, but she ignored it. "If you have a sister," she said skeptically, "why have you never mentioned her? Where has she been all this time?"

Cole looked at the ground, shoved his hands deep into his pockets, and started kicking at a rock buried in the mud. For a moment, Claire didn't think he was going to answer her, but then his voice softly floated across the prairie land.

"She is my half-sister. My father, well, you know," he looked up at her. "She has always had a little bit of a wilder streak, but heaven help me, I can't help but love her."

Claire raised her eyebrows, knowing there was more coming, but making sure she gave the cowboy all the space he needed. If nothing else, then to make up for her ridiculous adventure the night before, or for throwing his jacket on the ground – which still lay forgotten behind them.

"Don't say anything," he looked into her eyes, and she nodded her agreement. Only then did he continue. "A while back, she got into some trouble, drinking and partying, probably drugs. The whole scene. When she asked for money to go to rehab, I couldn't say no. I had to give her the chance that my father would never give himself."

Claire's heart melted. Of course, of course, he would put himself at risk to save his sister. "That's why you don't have the money to keep making payments on the ranch." It wasn't a question.

Cole nodded, looking at her with those big gentle eyes. "It wasn't a good situation to begin with. All the ranches around here have fallen on hard times. But that did in what little savings I had."

"I'm so sorry," Claire whispered as she studied the ground. "I wish there was something, anything, I could do to help."

"It's worth it." Cole's voice was soft again, and Claire brought her eyes up to meet his. "It was definitely worth it. Julie is doing much better now."

Claire went to him and hugged him, her arms around his middle, half because she wanted the comfort and half because she wanted to comfort him. His arms slid around her, and he sighed. "How are we going to get you home?"

Claire thought about it for a moment, and then said, "If you were a real cowboy, you would pick me up and carry me all the way back!"

Before the last words were completely out of her mouth, Cole's arms moved to brace her back and sweep up her legs from behind her knees. Claire squealed and threw her arms around his neck as she dissolved into laughter.

"Put me down!" she shouted and kicked her legs. "Put me down, you fool!"

Cole's entire body was shaking with laughter as he slowly lowered her back to the ground, careful of her ankle as he set her down. "I'm just trying to live up to your expectations."

Claire took a swat at his shoulder as she got her footing. "I'll be just fine, but lend me your arm to lean on. And don't forget that jacket." She nodded behind him.

Cole grabbed the jacket and then gallantly offered his arm up to Claire. "May I escort you to the ball, ma'am?" His voice held a tone of merriment. When Claire took his arm without a word, he pretended to be shocked. "No? Seven Brides for Seven Brothers?"

Claire shook her head, at a complete loss as to what the man was talking about.

He laughed. "Your film education is seriously lacking."

"Oh please," Claire said, rolling her eyes. "You probably haven't seen a movie that was made after 1960."

"That's not true. *Man From Snowy River*, 1982. One of my favorites."

Claire only rolled her eyes, again, in response. "Shall we?"

"Yes, we shall."

Claire leaned heavily on Cole as they hobbled back to the ranch, in no small part because she enjoyed the feel of him against her, but also because of her ankle. It wasn't sprained as bad as she had initially thought. However, they took it real slow, just to be safe. Or to enjoy each other's company. It didn't really matter which was true, not to Claire.

When the ranch house finally did come into view, they could see Julie standing on the porch. As soon as she spotted them, she ran down the stairs, headed straight for them.

"I was so worried," she yelled as she ran. "Are y'all crazy staying out all night?"

"Couldn't be helped," Cole said. Claire didn't have much to contribute, so she just smiled at the cowboy's sister.

As soon as Julie was within range, she threw her arms around Claire. "Hi! I've heard so much about you!"

Claire gave Cole a look over the girl's shoulder. He shrugged, the picture of innocence. Before Claire could think of anything to say, Julie had hooked her arm through Claire's, so that the tourist was in the middle of a Montana sandwich. "I want to hear all about your books and how you come up with the ideas, and just everything!"

Claire threw another glance at Cole, but the grin on his face told her everything she needed to know. He wasn't going to help her one bit. She tried the best she could to answer all the questions as they made their way to the house. Julie kept up a steady chatter the whole way. Claire didn't mind one bit, not with Cole's arm around her.

25. The Ranch

Her face, upturned to his, with tears gathering in her eyes, was enough to rip his heart out. Cole reached up with his right hand and tucked a piece of hair behind Claire's ear. This woman had turned his life upside down and on its ear, and now it was time for her to leave.

He had loaded her oversized suitcases into her tiny rental car, hating every second of it and half fantasizing about sabotaging the Smart-car. But now they stood next to the open driver's door, not sure what to say or do or even think. Julie had said goodbye in the house, but Cole was sure she was peeking out of some window somewhere. His sister had glommed onto Claire, and Cole couldn't say he was sad about it. Somehow, they had seemed right for each other.

The tourist, that damned tourist. She was looking up at him with the big brown eyes and with everything in him he wished he could somehow make her stay. They'd had a wonderful time in the days following the storm. Days that had been full of cooking together and cuddling in front of the fireplace. But her editor had called. Claire was needed back in the city. Though why in the day and age of the internet a writer couldn't be where she wanted, Cole didn't exactly understand. Maybe it was because he had never had anything installed on the ranch. Stupid technology.

He pulled Claire into his arms, holding her tightly and never wanting to let go. He could feel her tears soaking through his light button up shirt. He nuzzled his nose into her hair and breathed in deeply.

"Are you sure you don't want me to come with you to the airport?" he asked one last time.

"You know that won't work with the rental car and all," she choked out around the tears. Cole sighed. Of course, he knew. He just didn't like it – didn't like it one little bit.

"It's easier to say goodbye here, anyway," Claire assured him, pulling back slightly to look up into his face. Cole nodded. He wasn't sure of that logic either. "We'll talk, and email, and whatever," Claire said. "Keep the summer fling going as long as we want it to." She was trying to sound confident and sure, but Cole knew she was just as upset by the departure as he was.

Cole nodded but held his guest just a little tighter. "Summer fling," he murmured, not sure at all that was what this was, for either of them. They were so good for each other. It could have been more, so much more.

"I'll call you when I get back," Claire said, wiping the tears from her eyes, trying not to mess up her eye makeup, which was already all sorts of smudged.

"Yeah, that'd be good." Cole didn't loosen his grip on her.

"I have to go, Cole," Claire said softly, stepping back, forcing him to let go.

"Yeah," Cole said again. He felt like one of those suckers from a romantic comedy or something. The ones that cry all over themselves when the girl leaves. He stood straighter and rubbed at one of his eyes. He was not going to let himself fall apart like some sucker. It was only a summer fling after all.

Claire dipped herself into the tiny rental car, which was still smeared with dirt and dried mud from her arrival. Cole couldn't help but smile to himself. Who would have thought it would turn out that they could tolerate, even like each other, much less whatever it was that had grown between them. Claire got herself arranged in the car, and then Cole closed the door. She immediately rolled down the window.

"Thank you," she said, almost shyly. "Thank you for everything. I just... Thank you." Her words sounded choked at the end. Cole swallowed hard.

"Yes, ma'am," was all he could think to say. He took a step back from the car, which took all of the willpower he could muster. A fresh wave of tears began to roll down Claire's face, and she threw the car in reverse, a little harder than necessary. Cole almost winced, but he was still fighting to keep his own emotions under control.

The little car whipped around and plowed down the driveway. Cole waved, but he doubted Claire was watching for it. She was tearing herself out of his life. Perhaps she thought a quick break was best, and maybe it was. But that didn't help the boulder that settled in the pit of his stomach.

Cole whistled for Buck, who came running, and then set off to do the chores. He prayed they would distract him from the gaping hole that had appeared in his heart.

* * *

25. The Ranch

It was getting on to dusk and Cole was still working around the ranch. No matter how hard he worked, or how much he sweat, or how many times he looked in the direction of the guest cabin, he could not stop thinking of Claire. Buck seemed to feel the same way because the poor pup hadn't taken his eyes off of the driveway since she had disappeared down it.

"Well," Cole said as he pushed back his hat and wiped at the sweat beading there, "I guess we will have to try and get over her, Buck. To a certain degree at least."

Buck raised his head enough to look Cole in the eye with his own big, mopey eyes, and then laid back down to stare at the driveway.

"I know, buddy. I know." The words tasted bitter in his own mouth. He forced himself to think about other things. He should check with the realtor to see if there was any news with the listing. "Because thinking about one heartbreak over the other is so helpful," he murmured to himself.

Out of the corner of his eye, Cole caught a glance of Julie. She came tearing into the yard on the back of Scout. Just like a bat out of hell. Cole turned toward her, about to give her a real piece of his mind, but she beat him to it.

"Cole! You have to come! Right now!" Each word flew out of her mouth faster, louder, and higher pitched than the last. Cole had never seen her act like this before. Well, maybe when he gave her a Surge soda when she was eight, but that was a whole different kind of thing. Half of him almost worried that she was on something again. The poor girl could find that kind of stuff, even this far out in the country, if she really wanted to. But Cole quickly pushed the thought aside. She wouldn't, and this didn't seem like that kind of excitement anyway.

"What is going on?" His voice was tight with confusion. He

was tired, and more than tired, he was weary. But it hadn't escaped his notice that Buck had jumped up and was standing at attention, ears perked and staring down the driveway.

Julie swung off the stallion and walked toward Cole holding the reins. "I went for a ride."

"Clearly," Cole said dryly, his confusion and weariness mounting by the second. Julie rolled her eyes at him, just like she had when she was a teenager.

"Shut up. Listen to me!"

Yup, Cole thought to himself, still not sure what the subject of her excitement was, just like when she was a teenager.

Julia placed herself directly in front of him, one hand on her hip and the other still holding out Scout's reins. "Someone is messing with your sign!"

Cole stood still, stunned for a moment before the words sunk all the way in. This was Montana, where people left their front doors unlocked and the keys in the ignition of their vehicles. And now someone was vandalizing his for-sale sign? It didn't make sense. Unless Mr. Foster had put someone up to it. That bastard. As if Cole's emotions weren't strung out enough for the day.

Before he could give it another thought, he jerked the reins out of Julie's hands and quickly mounted Scout, who started sidestepping with nervous energy. Cole didn't say a word but turned the horse one-hundred-eighty degrees and then tapped him with the heels of his boots. They went flying down the driveway without a backward glance, leaving a trail of dust to follow them.

Cole worked to keep his mind clear, trying not to jump to conclusions. But his blood boiled nonetheless. The wind and speed of their flight did not cool his temper one bit. It might, in fact, be increasing it. Fanning the flames, so to speak. It occurred to Cole that he might have needed something like this to direct his anger at. No, he wasn't even going to try and hold it back. The anger would push Claire out of his head, for little a while, at least.

Scout was closing the distance to the end of the driveway at lightning speed, eager and willing to give into Cole's insistent nudging. The criminal was a small speck on the horizon, but Cole squinted, trying to make the man out. The devil was trying to wrench the for-sale sign from the ground.

Cole saw red. He pushed Scout even harder and started yelling at the top on his lungs, long before he was in earshot of the man. "You son of a gun! Leave my sign be! I'll have you thrown in jail for this!"

But at about a hundred yards out, Cole reined Scout to a sharp stop, causing the horse to rear up a little. What he saw at the sign stunned him.

It was a woman in a white t-shirt and blue jeans. Her hair danced in the light breeze. She was trying to rock the post of the for-sale sign and was failing miserably at it. She half gave up and began kicking at the sign.

Cole let out a deep laugh in both wonderment and delight. Claire whipped herself around to face him, her face full of determination and spunk.

"What in God's name are you doing?" Cole swung down from Scout's back and walked quickly toward the woman. With his anger evaporated into thin air, he finally noticed the little rental car parked in the middle of the driveway, her suitcases still taking up most of the tiny car's interior space.

"Well," Claire said a little sheepishly, kicking the sign behind her one more time, "I... ah... I may have done something a little impulsive."

Cole chuckled again, just happy to see her, but also vaguely aware this meant he would have to find the strength to say goodbye. Again. He decided he didn't care. He was going to be right here, in this moment. The rest be damned.

"I appreciate your impulsiveness," he said, a smile still lighting his face. "But that sign has to stay until the property is sold."

"About that." Claire wouldn't meet his eyes. She kicked at some pebble in the dirt Cole couldn't see. The sun was starting to set, casting everything in a glowing haze, and was quickly being pushed out by the dark blue night.

"About what?" Cole didn't really care what, his heart was beating too fast.

"I might..." she said a few more words, but so mumbled that Cole couldn't make them out. He dropped Scout's reins, knowing the horse would stay where it was, and moved closer to the beautiful tourist. He was within arm's reach when he stopped in front of her. She was still looking at the ground.

"I didn't catch that mumble," he teased, reaching one hand toward her arm.

She looked up and met his eyes then. There was a light dancing there, a light that both excited and terrified Cole.

"I may have bought the ranch."

Cole was sure he heard wrong, but his jaw dropped nonetheless. "Excuse me?" His words were a breathless whisper.

"I bought it." She was searching his face for some sort of response – approval, anger, Cole didn't know. Hell, he didn't even know what his response was. Everything suddenly felt blank.

"I don't understand." The words felt like peanut butter stuck in his throat. Was this some kind of a dream? "You bought

Paradise Valley Ranch?"

"Yes," Claire breathed her response, a wonderful smile taking over her face. "I needed a new investment."

Cole was in shock. What a day, he thought to himself.

"I know you will be happy with her," he said. He found that he was thrilled someone who would care about the land had bought it. He smiled. Claire must have massively undersold her novels if she could afford to buy at the asking price. Cole moved to hug her, smiling, happy and yet a little sad at the same time. Such was life, he supposed.

Claire melted into his arms willingly. It felt good, and he held her tight, nuzzling his head into her neck. By heaven, she smelled good.

"I'll try to get things taken care of pretty quick," he said, "So you can get on with whatever plans you have for it."

Claire pulled back from his arms, staring up at him with a perplexed look on her face. Cole rushed on; he needed her to know he was happy that she had bought it.

"I am thrilled my family's land is in good hands." He tried to pull her close again, feeling a loss at the distance she had put between them.

The tourist's brows furrowed even deeper. Her eyes screwed up in confusion. She didn't let him pull her back into a hug. Cole was starting to feel concerned when her face suddenly broke and the light returned to her eyes. She slugged him on the arm, hard, without any kind of warning.

"Hey!" Cole shouted, surprised, and rubbed his arm. "What was that for?"

"You are a damn fool, Patrick Cole." She just smiled up at him for several moments. He felt utterly confused and lost. "Obviously, you are still going to run the ranch."

Those words felt like a one-two straight to his gut.

"Don't think of it like I'm your boss," she teased, taking a step toward him so that they were almost nose to nose. "I'm more of a financial backer."

"Are you serious?" Cole asked, disbelief coloring every syllable.

"Yes!" Claire said, forcing herself back into his arms. "I am very, very serious." Her voice dropped down, and somehow it was even sexier than normal. "Of course," she said coyly, "I'm hoping you'll let me come stay every once in a while."

Cole finally lost it. He picked her up and started swinging her in a circle while letting loose a few first-rate rodeo hollers. Scout whinnied and pawed at the ground with a front hoof, wanting to join in on all the excitement. Claire laughed and squealed, happiness beaming off of her.

The sun was almost completely hidden behind the mountains, casting brilliant purples and pinks into the scattered clouds. A brighter star or two began to poke out in the darkening eastern sky. It was picture perfect. And Cole's heart was full to bursting. He put Claire down but didn't let her go.

"Are you sure?" he asked, searching her sparkling eyes.

"I've never been more sure of anything in my life," she answered. "Except maybe this." Claire pulled his head down and kissed him. A sweet, long, romantic kiss that got Cole's blood boiling. He held her tight and didn't let go until they were both breathless.

"This calls for a victory shot, don't you think?" Claire asked, her breath still coming in small, little pants.

"I do believe you are right, Boss Lady," Cole said.

"Oh no," she said, shaking her head, hands on hips. "You can't give me a title like that."

"Sure can. And you are just going to have to live with it." He couldn't help but tweak her nose, and she slugged him in the arm again as payback.

Cole grabbed her hand. "I guess the only way to stop that is to hold your hand," he teased.

"I guess so." Claire shrugged with all of the innocence in the world. "Let's go home."

Cole squeezed her hand, and she pressed back. They both felt happier than they could ever remember and they knew it was because they were together. Not just for a few weeks, not just a summer fling, but forever and always.

Without another word, they turned and started down the dirt road toward home, toward the mountains, and toward the glorious setting sun.

The End

The End

_Buy Long Way Home_to continue with this new chapter of love at Paradise Valley Ranch!

About the Author

Jana M. Floyd currently lives in the frozen tundra of Minnesota, but her heart will always belong to the Rocky Mountains of Montana.

Please visit janamfloyd.com to sign up for Jana M. Floyd's mailing list and get links to all her social media.

Also by Jana M. Floyd

Long Way Home
The Paradise Valley Series, Book Two

Rebekah
A Ghost Story